Braver Than Yesterday

A Novel

M. ROSE BUSHÉY

*P*rologue

*H*er name was Olivia; she had dark chestnut hair, eyes that were the color of the ocean so blue. She was the envy of every girl in high school. She was the captain of the swim team and the president of the student council. She had the looks, the brains, and she was the most popular girl. She had a lot of friends, but she still felt alone. Something inside her was missing, and it ate at her all day and night. Olivia got up for school, brushed her teeth, took a shower and grabbed something quick to eat that her mother made for her. She hurried out the door, didn't even bother giving them a kiss good bye. She just felt tired of the world, but she didn't show it. She kept it inside. She thought to herself, "Today is the day I'm going to do it; I'm going to commit suicide."

*O*ne

*O*livia walked up the street knowing where she was heading. She couldn't think anymore, she was tired of it. As she got to the covered bridge, she leaned over and saw that the water was high tide and it was moving pretty fast. She looked around and saw no one and right then and there she decided that she was going to jump. As she closed her eyes and was about to take the leap, someone grabbed her and pulled her to safety. Olivia looked up and saw this beautiful face in front of her. She couldn't decipher whether it was real or her imagination.

Then she heard a voice, "Hey there, are you alright?" All Olivia could do was stand there and say nothing she was in shock, he was beautiful, his eyes were dark brown and his hair was so dark and shiny like licorice. His face was angelic; she never saw something or someone so beautiful in her life.

"I was just breathing in the scent of the river," Olivia felt her face turn red.

"I think it was more than that, my name is Chris by the way, and you are?"

"Um, my name is Olivia." Chris helped her up, she just stood there feeling embarrassed.

"It's okay you don't have to worry, I'm not going to say anything to anyone, I couldn't let you do whatever you were going to do, just happen."

"I'm sorry." Olivia exclaimed, "You don't know me at all, you have no idea what's going on in my life and if I want to take the short way out of life, so be it".

Chris just looked at her and made a little grin, "If that's what you want to do, then go for it. I'll stand here and keep watch."

Olivia felt irritated, "Do you mind I rather be here by myself?"

"I can't just leave, I'm a witness now, I have to stand here and watch," Chris said.

"Fine," she said. She turned around, closed her eyes, and took a deep breath she was just about to jump again, but he grabbed her again.

"Why did you do that," she yelled.

"I can't just let you jump; you're life can't be that bad that you want to ruin it." Olivia stared at him and she could feel it right in her chest that she was going to cry. She tried not to but she couldn't control the emotions coming out of her. Chris grabbed her and hugged her tight. She didn't really know him, but she felt at that moment that he was going to be something special to her from that moment on.

*T*wo

Chris and Olivia became inseparable from that moment on. When Olivia had to go to swim practices or go to a match, he was there. It was as if he was her guardian angel. Olivia found out that Chris wasn't in high school; he graduated the previous year from a high school in Pennsylvania. She also found out that Chris moved there after his parent's split up. His mother moved down here to Asheville. He has a sister, LeAnn, and a brother, Johnny. They decided to stay with good old dad, mainly because he let them do whatever they pleased. His mother needed a shoulder to cry on so Chris felt it was necessary to come with her. Olivia's parents didn't approve of her hanging out with an older boy but Olivia didn't care what they thought, she needed him.

One day, Chris and Olivia decided to go to an orchard outside of town. They packed a picnic, lay down, and talked about their dreams.

"Olivia what do you want out of life?"

"I don't know, I guess just be happy, maybe to fall in love, get married, have children, the whole deal, how about you?"

"I feel like I want the same things." At that moment Olivia felt like she wanted to kiss Chris. They have never done anything of the sort. They would mainly hang out and maybe flirt with each other, but the idea of kissing or anything like that never came across to her. She looked up at him and she saw that he was just staring at her. Olivia felt a little funny inside. It was something she had never felt before. It was like excitement mixed in with nervousness.

"Olivia, can I ask you something?"

"Sure," she said.

"Can I kiss you?" Olivia couldn't believe her ears, she was just thinking that exact same thing but she didn't want to say anything.

"Okay," she said nervously. Chris leaned down and kissed her, it was Olivia's first kiss. She swore she heard fireworks.

"Wow that was really something," Chris said.

"Yeah it really was; I've never kissed anyone before." Chris leaned down again and kissed her, he laid down beside her. They were thinking the same exact things and felt in sync with one another; Olivia they were meant for each other.

*T*hree

*C*hris wouldn't let Olivia out of his sight. All they wanted was to be with each other. Although Olivia had her swimming, which she of enjoyed. When Chris came along she was thinking about quitting the team. She never told anyone because it didn't really mean anything to her anymore. She had a lot of girlfriends but it was like she couldn't talk to them about anything. Chris would come out to her practices and watch her; Olivia's friends thought that it was kind of creepy for him to watch.

"Hey Liv."

"Hey Jess, what's up?"

"I see your boyfriend is here again watching you."

"Doesn't that bother you just a little?" Olivia just laughed it off and shook her head.

"Of course not he loves me."

Olivia decided to go over Chris' house after swim practice, she went over there plenty of times but she still has yet to meet his mother.

"How come your mom is never here Chris?"

"She's always working to pay the bills."

"How come you don't work and help her out?" Chris looked at her with an evil look, she immediately regretted saying that.

"I don't need to work. I want to be here with you and look after you." Chris gave her a look that sent chills down her spine, "Don't ever say anything to me like that ever again!" Chris automatically swung his arm back and hit her on her left side of her face. Olivia fell back and started crying. Chris right away felt bad and ran to her, he kissed her and apologized. "I'll never do that again Liv, I promise I love you so much."

"I love you too Chris but why did you do that?"

"I'm sorry I just wasn't thinking, I will never do that again." Chris started kissing her, soothing her. He started unbuttoning her shirt.

"Chris wait I don't know if I'm ready."

"It's okay baby we can wait, I just love you so much."

"I just never had sex before."

"I haven't either; I just thought it would be special." Chris convinced Olivia. He started to unbutton her shirt and he was kissing her gently on her lips and then moved down to her neck. Olivia thought it felt amazing and her heart was beating so fast. Chris took off her shirt and started feeling her chest. They were so firm and they felt good in his hands. Olivia was starting to breath heavy, she felt him up against her. She was really nervous but also very excited. Olivia sat up to take off her bra. "Are you sure you want to do this Liv?"

"Yes Chris, I trust you." He gently kissed and felt her chest. She was going out of her mind. She was wearing a skirt and Chris took his hand and went under her skirt and started cupping her. He slowly took off her skirt. He started to kiss her more passionately on the mouth and made his way down to her stomach. Olivia tried to take off his clothes; she pulled off his shirt and was kissing his chest. She wanted this to be special because this was her first time.

He pulled her down on the bed slowly and put himself inside her. She started to wince, "Does it hurt baby?"

"A little."

"I'll try and go slow." He was very gentle with her, he thought it felt amazing. He wanted it so bad so he started to go a little faster. "I'm almost done baby, relax." Olivia couldn't relax because it was starting to hurt. Chris wouldn't stop and he decided to go even faster. Olivia started screaming for him to stop.

"Chris! Please stop!" He wouldn't stop; he held her down and just kept going. Finally he relaxed and went inside her.

"Now you're all mine baby!" Olivia didn't understand, she thought he was her one and only. The guy she was meant to be with.

"Chris what the hell was that all about it? I want to go home!"

"I'm sorry baby but you can't leave."

"What the fuck do you mean I can't leave?"

"You're never leaving me again," he said. Olivia was so confused she started screaming and tried to run, but he threw her back on the bed and started wailing on her. Olivia lay there not moving. It turned out that Chris was a psychopath!

*F*our

Olivia came to and sat up in the bed. She looked around the room but Chris was nowhere to be seen. She had no idea what was happening, all she knew was that she wanted to get out of there and go home. She walked over to the supposed window and moved the curtains to the side and she realized there wasn't a window. Olivia was scared and started to panic. She hurried over to the door and tried to open it and it was locked. She started to cry, scream and yell. Just then the door opened and Chris walked through the door. He grabbed her hair and threw her down on the bed.

"Why are you doing this Chris?" she asked.

"Liv I told you you're not leaving me ever again."

"What do you mean I'm not leaving? I need to go home." Chris was getting tired of her crying so he hit her hard in the face and she collapsed on the bed. Olivia couldn't believe what was happening. She started to believe she was being held captive. Chris walked over to her and pinned her down. Olivia gasped. "Chris, what are you doing?"

"You're going to give me what I want from now on." Olivia started screaming. Chris walked over to grab some tape that was in a drawer on the side of the room and taped her mouth shut. "You have to be a good girl now and do what you're told, if not then the tape stays! Do you agree Liv?" Olivia stood there stunned she didn't know what to do; she shook her head slowly. "Good girl, now I'm going to take off the tape." Chris pulled off the tape and told her to stand up. "Liv I want you to take off your shirt."

"But why?"

"I want to see you again."

"But you've already seen me."

"Stop talking and do what I tell you or I'll put the tape back on." Olivia did as Chris said. "Now take

14

off the rest of your clothes." Olivia started to cry, she was so scared. All she wanted to do was go home. Olivia decided to do what she was told and get undressed. "Good girl Liv, now I want you to turn around and kneel on the bed." Olivia did as she was told but knew deep down inside that this was wrong. What was he going to do?

All of a sudden she felt him against her, "He must've taken off his clothes," Olivia thought. The next instant she felt pain. He slammed himself inside her.

"Don't even think about screaming!"

"Please stop, I can't take anymore! I just want to go home!"

"I told you what would happen f you didn't listen to me, you're being a bad girl," he slammed himself inside her again. This time Olivia was quiet. She just knelt in silence but with tears streaming down her face.

Chris was feeling her chest and holding them tightly. Olivia was in so much pain.

"Now turn around I want to see that pretty face." Olivia had no choice but to turn around. She saw in his eyes something she had never seen. It was like he was a completely different person. He laid her back down and put himself inside her again. She winced in pain but she knew she had to take it. He started to scream her name and then he finished inside of her. He rolled off of her and kissed her forehead. "That was a good girl; I'll give you some food so you can get your energy up.

"Why are you doing this?"

"You're my girl Liv." He got up off the bed and left the room. Olivia worked up the energy to put her clothes back on. A few minutes later Chris brought some food for her, set it down on the bed and left. Olivia picked at the food and ate a little. She was so upset and scared.

As the day went on Olivia just sat there. She realized there was a bathroom in the corner of the room. She got up and used the toile and saw the shower. She turned the water on, took her clothes off and stood under the hot water. She suddenly felt like someone was watching her so she turned around and there he was.

"Are you feeling any better baby?"

"I just wanted to take a shower Chris." At first she didn't notice but then realized that he was naked. He went inside the shower with her and she slowly backed in the corner of the shower.

"Don't be scared Liv I'm here for you."

"How can you be here for me when you're holding me captive and won't let me leave?"

"I told you baby girl because you're mine." Olivia started to cover herself up she felt ashamed.

"Don't you dare cover yourself up, you're beautiful baby. I want to see all of you." He put her arms down and looked up and down at her body. Her breasts were so firm and round. Olivia looked shocked and embarrassed. She started to put her hands over herself and again he forced them down. He came over to her and started feeling them. She just stood there. "I want to make a baby with you Liv."

"What! That's crazy I don't even know you. I'm just a teenager."

"It's going to happen Liv, whether you want it or not. I'm sorry but I want one with you, you're the love of my life." Chris put himself inside her and finished. Olivia felt like she was trapped forever with this man who thought was the love her life.

*F*ive

*O*livia woke up and knew her parents were looking for her. She felt so stupid for neglecting them all the time. She knew then that they were right about Chris. She was thinking that they probably thought that she had run away with him. Her parents did know where he lived so she assumed that they would come looking for her there. A few times she thought she heard knocking at the door but nothing ever came of it. "I wonder what my parents are doing," she said out loud. She missed her friends and her swim team. She knew she had to get out of there but she didn't know how. Olivia heard the familiar walking down the steps and the unlocking of the door and Chris came in.

"Hey there baby. How are you doing?"

"I'm fine." She noticed the door was open a little and she thought maybe she could get away somehow. She walked up to Chris and hugged him tightly. "Let's dance Chris."

"But there's no music."

"We can make it up in our minds." They started swaying side to side. She put her head on his shoulder. When she got to where the door was she pushed him down on the bed and ran. It felt like she was running forever. She went to the stairs and ran to the top but she stopped when she saw another man in front of her. He grabbed her and held her there. "Please help, please help me!"

"Look at what we have here, nice young meat." Olivia then realized that this man was working with Chris. She turned around and there was Chris with a big grin on his face.

"I see you met Joe, Joe this is Olivia. '

"Pleased to make you're acquaintance cutie pie."

"What is this?" Olivia asked. Next thing she knew, Chris picked her up and brought her downstairs to the basement.

Chris turned and looked up at Joe, "Are you coming?"

"Hell yea man I want to see that pink little bottom." Chris threw her down on the bed and ripped her clothes off. "Wow, I don't think I've ever seen anything so beautiful in my life."

"Thanks bro. Hey if you want you can have her since we're both family." Joe didn't waste any time and took off his clothes. He pulled her down and flipped her over and lubricated her and forced himself inside of her. Olivia started to scream; Chris walked over and put the tape over her mouth. Chris felt like he was missing out on the action. He got undressed. "Move over bro, I want to get in on that." They both had Olivia over and over, even at the same time. By the end Olivia was a wreck and exhausted. They left the room and she passed out.

When Olivia came to, she didn't know where she was. She looked around and realized she was still there in the house with Chris and his cousin. She felt really sore so she hobbled to the bathroom and stripped her clothes off again and took a hot shower. By the time she was finished showering, she started to feel a little better. She started thinking about everything that she was missing in her life. She couldn't believe she was so naïve. She sat there and had to figure out a plan how to get out of there. She knew that if she stayed there any longer she would die.

Six

Days turned to weeks and Olivia was locked in the basement. Chris and Joe were coming for her every day.

One morning she got up and she felt sick. She didn't know why. She lay down on the bed and sometimes ran for the toilet to vomit.

Chris came in, "Are you alright?"

"I don't feel that great Chris."

"I'll be right back." He turned around and left the room. He came back a few minutes with what looked like a pregnancy test.

"What is this for?" Olivia asked.

"You might be pregnant Liv." Olivia didn't want to be, especially not with this guy. She hated him. Chris took her to the bathroom and told her to use it. She read the instructions on how to use it and then took the test. A few minutes later she got the results. "Well look at that, we're going to have ourselves a baby." Olivia felt sick to her stomach. She couldn't believe this was happening to her.

"What do we do Chris?"

"We are going to do nothing because we're going to have this baby."

"But I don't know anything about babies, I really don't want this."

"You're going to have this baby, it's ours." There was nothing for her to do she was stuck. She knew she needed to get out of there and she needed a plan. Over the next few days she would really pay attention to her surroundings. She noticed that Chris came and left like clockwork. Olivia also noticed that Joe wasn't coming around anymore. She thought maybe because she was pregnant now and Chris didn't want him to be around her. Chris was visiting her often now; he would come back a few times and give her books to read on pregnancy. Olivia knew that now that she was reading these books that she needed to get some vitamins to help the baby develop.

One night when Chris came in to check on her and to give her something to eat, Olivia asked him to get the vitamins.

"What do you need vitamins for?"

"It's for the baby Chris. Without them the baby won't be healthy and also one of the books says I need to see a physician to see if the baby and I are going to be alright." Olivia was hoping to get out of the house and somehow escape the monster.

"Liv, you know I can't let you leave the house."

"I know Chris but it's for our baby's sake, I want it to be healthy."

"I'm sorry you're going to have to stay here and hope for the best." Chris got up and headed for the door and slammed it. Olivia collapsed on the bed and cried. She felt like it was her only way out. She wanted to be back with her parents, she was so scared.

Day after day she stayed in this room without sunlight and no windows to look out of. It was like the world around her just vanished. Olivia figured there would be no hope and so every day she would pray for a miracle.

Seven

Olivia felt herself getting bigger. Chris wouldn't give her any clothes to wear, just a dress. She asked him one night where his mother was.

"My mother doesn't live here Liv, I'm here by myself." He never said what happened to her. Olivia thought to herself, "Did he kill her," nothing surprised her anymore. Sometimes she wished there were, at least there would be another woman here to help her and guide her. Chris left her alone most of the time; he threw himself upon her only when he was really frustrated.

One day she was sitting there on the bed and reading some of the books that Chris gave her when she heard shuffling. She thought maybe someone came for her, to rescue her. All of a sudden the door flew open and Chris threw a girl down on the bed.

27

"She has to be around my age," she thought. There was so much commotion, she was screaming and he was yelling. I just stared and moved into the corner where the bathroom was. She thought, "This could finally be my chance to get out of here." She started going towards the door when she noticed Joe appear. Olivia got scared, ran back into the room and in the corner again. She knelt down.

"That's a good girl," Joe said.

"Open wide for me." She shook her head no and started screaming, "Chris! Chris!" Chris turned around and saw what Joe was up too so he threw him out of the room.

"Leave my girl alone Joe!"

"Come on cuz I already had a slice of her; I wanted to see what those lips can do."

"I said back off or I'll give you something that you'll never forget."

Joe let it go and as he walked away he turned around and smirked and said, "One day pretty you'll be mine."

Chris just shook his head, "I'll make sure he leaves you alone Liv." Meanwhile the girl that came in is livid. She is sobbing hard. It's the same way Olivia felt a few months ago. She knew exactly what this girl was going through. "Go in the bathroom Liv."

"Why?"

"I don't want you to see this."

"See what?"

"Just go in the bathroom!" Olivia did what she was told but she could hear everything. The girl was screaming for him to get off of her but Chris smacked her in the face and then it got quiet. Olivia peered through the door to see what was happening; she looked and saw Chris standing over her. Joe was there too and he started taking off the girl's clothes. Olivia wanted to yell for them to get off of her but she didn't dare. Then she saw both of the guys taking off their clothes and one by one they took turns on her. She felt horrible; her heart sank into her chest. They were doing the same thing to that girl that they did to her. The last thing Chris said to her was, "I want you to have my baby." Olivia thought, "oh my God, not her too."

They got of the girl and slammed the door behind them. Olivia started to come out of the bathroom and walk over to the girl.

"Hey, are you okay?" The girl looked up at Olivia, her face was tear stained.

"Who are you?" the girl asked.

"My name is Olivia, what's your name?"

"I'm Joy, what are you doing here, what is happening?" Olivia felt sorry for this girl; she knew that she was feeling how she felt when she was first abducted.

"I knew Chris for awhile and we became really close, I thought I was in love with him. Next thing I knew we came here to this house and he wouldn't let me leave." Olivia started to get tears in her eyes. "Chris and his friend Joe would take turns with me just like they did with you. Now I'm pregnant."

"Oh my God you're pregnant?"

"What if that happens to me? Is that what they're trying to do?"

"Honestly Joy, I really have no idea what their plan is."

"I've been down here for a few months now."

Olivia and Joy became fast friends; they had each other to keep company. Joy would fall asleep but Olivia would hear her having horrible nightmares. She was crying out and screaming. Olivia usually had to go over to her and comfort her. Olivia knew they had to get out of there but she didn't know how they were going to manage it. Every day the same things occurred, Chris and Joe would come in and take their turn with Joy. She would put up a good fight until they hit her until she was unconscious or until she lay there silent.

"Chris, why don't you leave her alone?"

"Mind your business Liv or you'll be next!" Olivia covered her ears and shut her eyes; it was the only way to shut out the horror.

*E*ight

*O*livia couldn't believe how big she was getting. She assumed she was about five months along; time seemed to be flying by. Chris would come in and visit her occasionally but not as much as he would Joy. In a way Olivia was relieved, she didn't want to deal with him.

"Joy I'm going to get in the shower." Joy didn't say anything. Next thing she knew, Olivia saw a shadow reflected off the shower curtain, it was Chris.

"Wow baby you're getting so big."

"Well that's what happens when you have a baby in your stomach, you tend to get big."

"You're still as funny as ever with a smart ass mouth."

"Turn around," Chris said. Olivia knew she had to do what she was told because she didn't want any trouble. Now that she was far along in her pregnancy, she couldn't wait to meet her baby. It was the only thing she looked forward to. Chris grabbed the soap and lathered up the sponge and started rubbing her body. "Your tits are still nice and firm and very full." Chris started to caress her chest; Olivia was rolling her eyes. She felt his naked body behind her.

"What are you doing Chris?"

"You know what I'm going to do."

"But what about the baby, I don't think it's a good idea."

"I don't care what you think; you're going to take what I'm going to give you." Olivia was forced to bend over and Chris put himself in her, he was moaning loudly. "You being pregnant is making this so much hotter." Olivia couldn't believe what she was hearing, "He's a complete psychopath," she thought.

After he was finished he walked out of the shower and Olivia just slid to the floor crying. Olivia could now hear crying and screaming. He was now having his way with Joy. After Olivia heard the door slam, she got up off the floor, grabbed a towel and walked over to Joy who was lying there sobbing.

"Are you okay Joy?"

"I want to get out of here, I want my mom."

"I know me too, I miss them."

"How did you meet him Joy?"

"I was at the county fair with my friends and we were just walking around when we bumped into a few guys. Chris was one of them and so was Joe." The way Olivia's face lit up, she could tell Chris put on his act just like he did for her. "We started talking and he was so gorgeous, those eyes and that hair. Anyway, we started hanging out and we became inseparable. One night Chris took me to this farm and it was secluded and he made it romantic, there were lights everywhere and there was a blanket with a picnic. I couldn't help think how romantic it was, so we sat down and ate and talked about everything. There was a bottle of champagne and I told him I wasn't old enough to drink. He said that it would be all right and that he just wanted to make a toast to us. So he poured me a glass and we toasted to new beginnings. I drank that down and he poured me another, I was iffy of course but I drank that glass too. I started to feel a little funny and giggly. Next thing I knew he was on top of me taking off my clothes. I told him I wasn't ready but he said he would be gentle. So I let him and next thing I know he was inside me, I was a virgin." Joy looked like she was about to cry so Olivia put her arm around her.

"How did you get here?"

"He told me he wanted me to meet his mother, he told me I was the one and that we were going to get married. Boy was I wrong; I fell for his stupid charm. When I got here, he said there was a surprise for me in the basement and took me down here." Joy was really sobbing now and Olivia hugged her tightly and whispered to her, "We will get out of here."

The next day, Olivia woke up and didn't see Joy but realized she heard her in the bathroom throwing up. That's when Olivia knew she was pregnant too and Chris had done what he said he was going to do. Joy came out of the bathroom with an ashy face.

"I don't know what's wrong with me," she said.

"Joy I think that you're pregnant. How do you feel?"

"Oh no, I don't want to be pregnant!" Joy started to cry hysterically. Olivia had to be strong for her and to tell her it was going to be okay. They heard the door unlock and Chris came in.

"What's going on in here?"

"It looks like you may have to get another test; I think you got Joy pregnant. Well done."

Chris looked over at Joy and smiled, "I'll be right back." He left the room and grabbed another test. He came back and handed her the test, "Here take it." Joy grabbed the test, took it and it was positive. She gave the test back to Chris, "Now you're all mine too baby."

Joy started screaming, "I don't want this baby!! I want to go home."

Chris replied, "You're never leaving me again." It was the same thing he had said to Olivia.

Nine

Over the next few days, Chris got her the vitamins that Joy needed for the baby. He told her to read the books that he gave Olivia.

"Um Chris," Olivia said, "When it's time to have this baby, you're taking me to the hospital right?"

"Sorry Liv can't do that."

"What do you mean? Are you going to deliver this baby, do you even know how?"

"One day at a time Liv." And with that he left the room. Olivia sat down on the bed.

"Is he nuts or something to think that I can have this baby by myself?"

"Liv you already know he is nuts so it shouldn't surprise you."

"I know but this is another human beings life we're talking about."

"When it comes down to it I'll help you; I know you would do the same thing for me. We're here for each other." Both Joy and Olivia felt better knowing they had each other to look after. Knowing that they had to get out of there because of both of them being pregnant, they searched thoroughly throughout the room. They checked under the bed, the walls, and the ceiling. They discovered that there wasn't any possible way to escape. Hope escaped both of them. Chris would visit frequently to make sure that they were fed and to make sure they were okay health wise.

"How are my soon to be mommies?"

"We're fine, but would really like to get out of here so we can get real care. We don't even know if the babies are healthy," said Olivia.

"They will be fine Liv, don't worry about that."

"I don't get why you even want to have these babies with us."

"Don't you get it darling, you're my girl and that is my child, we are now one. Same thing goes for you Joy."

"I really thought you were the one Chris." Joy cried.

"I am the one Joy; you're just not seeing the bigger picture. We're going to have a family and be a whole unit." Both girls just stared at him. "Joy I think it's time you go into the shower, you're hair needs a good washing, I'll be in in a minute."

"I don't need a shower Chris, I'm clean and I just got a shower." Chris smacked her across the face and yelled at her to get in the bathroom. Joy cried all the way to the bathroom and shut the door.

Chris looked at Olivia, "You're getting so big Liv it's almost that time." Chris bent over and started to feel her belly and slowly moved down to her crotch. Olivia pushed his hand away. "Don't push my hand away, unless you want to get smacked!"

"No! I just know it's not a good time."

"For saying that I'll go and take it all out on Joy, is that what you want?"

"No, of course I don't want you to do that!"

"Open wide for me then." He forced himself in Olivia's mouth to get him worked up; he took his hand and went between her legs. When he was done with Olivia, he walked into the bathroom. It was quiet except for the water running.

"Hello Joy, are you ready for me? You didn't undress? I want you out of those clothes and into the shower." Joy did as she was told. He grabbed the shampoo and massaged her head. She forgot for one second where she was, that was until he forced his tongue into her mouth. He stepped back from her and looked her up and down. "Your body is amazing Joy, I could stare at it all day." He reached up to her chest and felt that they too were full. She saw that he was bending down and took her in his mouth. She didn't want this but she didn't have a choice. Joy starting moaning, she couldn't help. He stuck a finger in and out of her. He stood up, "You like that baby?" Joy just shook her head. "Good, now turn around." He forced himself inside her and started pounding, she screamed out. After a minute or two he was finished and left her standing there soaked and confused.

Chris walked out of the bathroom and looked at Olivia, "I think I found my new favorite." Olivia didn't care; she didn't want anything to do with this man. Joy walked out of the bathroom with a towel on, Olivia handed her some clothes.

"Are you okay?" Olivia asked.

"I'm okay; it's strange though one minute I'm standing there and didn't want anything to do with him and then the next I wanted him. I don't know what the hell that means."

"It doesn't mean anything Joy; it just means that you have given up and you let him have you."

"I worry about the baby when he does things like that, it can't be good for them."

"I agree but I don't know what else we can do. We can't convince him otherwise. Joy sat down on the bed and then looked up at Olivia.

"Liv you never mentioned how you and Chris met."

"I never really wanted to talk about it I guess."

"Would you mind telling me?"

"Sure why not. We met actually when I was going to commit suicide."

Joy looked shock, "What really?"

"Yea I thought I was having a bad time in my life and I was depressed. I couldn't take it anymore and thought that ending my life would really help. Anyway, I went to a covered bridge around my house and just stood there staring at the rushing water. I thought to myself that I needed to end this life and that's when Chris came along and pulled me off the edge. He basically talked me out of it. After that we became inseparable, just like how you and he were."

"So how did you end up here?"

"Well we didn't have sex yet. I was a virgin just like you were and he wanted me to come back here, so I did. We ended up having my first time on this bed and I haven't left since."

"How long have you been here?"

"I've been here for six months and counting. I got pregnant right away I think right after Chris and his cousin double tagged me." Olivia looked as if she was going to cry, but she knew she had to be stronger than that, especially for Joy.

"Oh Olivia, I had no idea you were here that long. You know now that I recall, I kind of remember a story in the paper about a missing girl. The whole town was looking for her. That must've been you."

"Really, they were looking for me? Olivia cried.

"Yea I vaguely remember that, it was on the news. Your parents were looking frantically for you."

"They didn't question Chris?"

"I think they mentioned something about a boyfriend but he checked out."

"I guess you never know huh?" Olivia just stared at the wall; she couldn't believe that they were actually looking for her. She thought they didn't care about her. At that moment she knew she had to get of there, and be stronger than before.

*T*en

Olivia was planning her escape. She had no idea why Chris was keeping her and Joy here and why he wanted them to have his babies, beside the reason he gave them before. She felt so much love for the baby growing inside of her; she didn't want anything to happen to it. She looked furiously through the room to find something she could turn into a weapon or something that could break the lock on the door. She found some string, a hanger, and some things that Chris left for both of them, which she collected throughout her stay.

"Joy, we are getting out of here. We need to take care of ourselves and our babies."

"What if something happens and Chris catches us? He'll kill us."

"I'm sorry Joy but that's a risk I'm willing to take, he could kill us anyway." Olivia decided that night she was going to try and escape. As evening fell, Olivia told Joy the plan. She would break the lock and they would get away together. They both knew that Chris wouldn't be coming back for the rest of the night, so Olivia started working on the door. It took hours before she figured out how to get it open. The door finally opened; Olivia felt a sense of freedom and panic. But mostly she felt adrenaline. Quietly she turned to Joy, "Come on we're leaving, and be quiet, that's all we need is asshole to find us. He probably would beat us to a bloody pulp." Joy got up off the bed and walked slowly and quietly towards Olivia.

Both girls walked out the door and into the basement. The room was really dark; they could barely see where they were going. To the right they didn't see anything but boxes, but to the left there were stairs that led up into the first floor of the house.

Olivia felt hesitant about going up; she didn't know what awaited them.

"We have to find another way out, Joy you go that way, and I'll go this way. Maybe there's a window we can get out of, and Joy please be careful and be quiet."

Joy whispered, "Okay". Both girls walked around the basement, looking for a window. Olivia thought she saw something by the wall. She walked over to it and sure enough covering a portion of the wall was a window it was covered by a cloth.

"Hey Joy, she whispered as loud as she could, I found a window." Joy tiptoed over to Olivia. She lifted the cloth and pulled it down. "Look for a box or something I can stand on. The window is a little too high, I can't reach it." They both looked around frantically. Joy found a bucket for Olivia to stand up on. Olivia stood up and looked out, she felt a sense of freedom, but was worried because she noticed that the sun was starting to rise. The sky looked like a purplish-pink. She thought it was the most beautiful sight she had ever seen. She tried to pry the window open and it wouldn't budge. "I can't open the window," cried Olivia. Joy looked around for something to try and open it.

"Liv, all I found was a blanket, why don't you hold it over the window and break the glass."

"Good idea Joy, hopefully it won't make any noise." Olivia took the blanket and held it over the window and she punched through the glass. They looked at each other and thought they heard a noise. They were quiet for what felt like a lifetime. They didn't hear anything else. Olivia removed the blanket and pulled herself through the window, she didn't see anything. The coast was clear. She reached for Joy and grabbed her; she was halfway through when she heard someone coming down the stairs, it was Chris.

"Oh my God, Chris is coming, hurry up and pull me out." Olivia pulled her out and they were free. Chris walked into the room, he had no idea they were gone.

He yelled "Shit!" He ran up the stairs and yelled for Joe to get up. They went outside and all he could see were two girls in the distance yelling and screaming.

*E*leven

Olivia and Joy found a house and banged on the door. A man answered the door and saw two girls pregnant and filthy. They were screaming and crying to call the police. The man got on the phone immediately and called 911. "The police are on their way, I called an ambulance too because I can see that you're both pregnant. Are you both alright, where did you come from?" Olivia was crying but she calmed down and told him everything. By the time she was finished, the police showed up. The police called their parents and let them know that they were safe and that they would be at Asheville Hospital. The girls were both going to the hospital by ambulance.

When they arrived, their parents met them. They were immediately taken back to the emergency room. The parents were there to greet them.

"Mom!" Olivia cried. Her parents hugged her, she was so happy to be back in their arms.

"What happened to you Olivia? Where were you, we thought you ran away." Olivia just broke down and cried.

"Mom I'm pregnant." Olivia's mom just cried and asked her what happened.

"It was Chris; he raped me and another girl Joy and kept us locked in his basement. He said he wanted to get us pregnant on purpose. He said we belonged to him." Just when her mom was going to say something, the doctor came in and wanted to take her up to make sure she was okay and to see how the baby was doing.

"Hi Olivia I'm Dr. Kravitz, I just wanted to take a look at your baby, do you mind if I do a little exam?"

"Can my mom be in the room for it?"

"Of course she can, I'll go and get her." When her mom came into the room the doctor started the exam. "I see a little tearing in your vagina and that it is consistent with rape, I'm going to take a few samples. She felt her hand inside her next. "Relax Olivia; I just want to make sure the baby is faced correctly which it feels like it is. Next I'm going to do the ultrasound. Let's lift up the gown here a little bit. I'm going to squirt this liquid on your abdomen; it might be a little cold." The doctor was looking intently at the ultrasound, making sure everything was as it should be. After the exam was over the doctor asked, "Would you like to know the sex of the baby?"

Olivia looked at her mom, "It's up to you Olivia."

"Sure, I would like to know."

"It's a girl and you'll be happy to know that she's healthy." Olivia couldn't believe her ears. She was so happy and tears started flowing. "You're about seven months pregnant so you have a few months to go. We would like to keep our eye on you just to be on the safe side."

"Do you know how my friend is doing?"

"You can go visit her if you'd like, she's in the room next door. I would just use the wheel chair to get over there; maybe your mom can wheel you over there." Olivia looked at her mom who helped her into the chair and wheeled her next door. When Olivia went into the room, she saw Joy and threw her arms around her. They were so happy to see each other.

"Hey Liv, this is my mom, Charlotte."

"Oh I'm so happy to meet you. Olivia was a life saver for me. This is my mom Caroline."

"Oh Joy, we were both life savers to each other." They said hello to each other and both moms left the room so they could talk and leave Joy and Olivia alone. "So did they tell you anything about the baby?" asked Olivia.

"Yeah they did the exam on me and they told me I'm having a boy, they said I was five months along. They said the baby was healthy, thank God. Did they tell you about your baby?"

"Yeah they said I was seven months pregnant and I was having a girl, and also the baby is healthy."

"What do you think happened to Chris?" asked Joy.

"I don't know I haven't heard anything."
When the girl's parents had returned they asked them if they heard anything about Chris or his cousin.

Both parents looked at each other and said, "They looked for them at the house and they weren't there. But they are looking for them; they have warrants for their arrest. Don't worry they'll find them."

The girls looked at each other; they were thinking the same thing, "What if he comes back?" Olivia hugged Joy and went back to her room to rest up. Tomorrow would be a new day.

*T*welve

*T*he sun was up and it was lighting up the hospital room, Olivia thought she never would see the sun again. Life has become more precious to her now that she was back safe and sound. She still worried however, if Chris was going to come back for her. She was after all carrying his child and she knew he wanted the babies and them.

"Hey mom, can I see Joy?"

"I don't know if she's awake yet honey. Why don't you eat some breakfast first and then you can go over and see her?" Olivia was disappointed but she listened to her and ate something. Olivia felt more energized the moment she ate, the food helped her. She could feel the baby moving around and she just laughed, she thought it was an amazing feeling. After breakfast, Olivia got up to see if Joy was awake yet, and sure enough she was.

"Hey Joy, how are you feeling?"

"I'm feeling alright Liv, how are you?"

"I'm doing great. Do you think we'll be able to go home today?"

"I don't know I'm hoping too."

"Hey Joy, I was wondering if we can make a pact, to always stay by each other's side no matter what."

"Of course Liv, I couldn't live without you, you basically saved my life." The girls were really good friends; they would try and visit with each other every chance they got. "Liv, can I ask you something?"

"Sure."

"Do you think you'll ever date again? '

"I don't know Joy, I feel like I'll have a hard time trusting anyone for awhile. I mean besides you of course."

"I feel the same way." That day they were both discharged from the hospital.

One night, Joy was over and they decided to have a sleep over, Olivia was getting so big and it was almost time for her to have the baby. She stayed in her bed a lot because she was so tired lately.

"I need to talk to you about something Joy."

"Sure Liv what's up?"

"I'm not sure if I want to put it out there or tell you."

"Olivia you know you can tell me anything."

"Okay fine." She laughed.

"I've been really happy that you're here for me and that we became really good friends." Joy felt the same way about her. "I don't know if I ever want to date anyone ever again. Please don't laugh at me or anything, I know it sounds crazy but I don't know if I'll ever be able to just trust anyone ever again with what happened to us."

"Liv in all honesty I feel the same way, I didn't want to say anything because I thought the same thing about it being crazy. You're the only one I trust to talk about these things and we've both been through the same experience, I think it just makes sense." Olivia looked relieved. I'm glad we're on the same page with each other and we can be totally honest."

"I love you Olivia." Olivia looked at Joy and told her she loved her too. What Joy didn't mention to Olivia was that she was secretly in love with her, she didn't know if she could ever bring herself to tell her, so she decided to keep it a secret for now. They held each other until they fell asleep. Olivia woke up in the middle of the night, her water broke, and she knew it was time.

"Joy wake up, I think it's time." Joy got up and rushed around the room trying to grab Olivia's things together and then she ran to wake up Olivia's parents. By the time they got to the hospital Olivia was screaming from contractions.

"It will be okay, just relax," said her mom. The doctor that she saw previously took her and her mom back into maternity. Joy waited patiently in the waiting room. What Olivia or Joy didn't know was that Chris and Joe were always around, stalking both of them. Joe was there at the hospital when Olivia went into labor. Joy was sitting in the waiting room when a man sat down next to her. She didn't think anything of it until something poked her in her side. Joy looked over her shoulder and saw that it was Joe. He had some facial hair, his hair was longer and he was wearing a hat.

"Long time no see Joy."

"What are you doing here?" Joy whispered. "You know the cops are looking for you, I could scream right now and they would take you away."

"I don't think so darlin', I don't think you would want to die would you?" Joy just looked scared as tears started to fill her eyes. "Let's go we're leaving and don't try and make a scene or else." Joy started to follow Joe when Olivia's mom appeared.

"Joy, where are you going? Don't you want to see the baby?"

"Oh yeah of course Mrs. Mallor, I just wanted to get some air, I'll be right back."

"Hey who's your friend?" Joy looked scared; she didn't know what to say.

"Oh hello ma'am, I'm Nick, Joy is my girlfriend."

"Girlfriend, I don't think she ever mentioned she was dating anyone."

"Really babe, you never mentioned me before?" Joy just shook her head.

"Are you okay Joy?" Caroline asked.

"She's fine, aren't you Joy?"

"Yes, I'm fine Mrs. Mallor." When Joy walked away and went outside with Joe, Caroline went to security and told him something looked a little off and to please check it out. The security guard went outside to check. He saw that the man was yelling at the girl and it looked like he had a gun.

He yelled at Joe, "Hey you there!"

Joe turned around and yelled back at the guy, "Mind your own business old man." The security guard got on his radio and told dispatch to call the police. Joe was trying to shove Joy into the car but she was fighting back. The security guard ran over to pull Joe off of her; Joe shot at the guard but missed. People in the waiting room heard the gunshots and were screaming. A police officer ran out of the room and ran outside; he saw the guard and Joe struggling.

"Drop your weapon!" the cop said. Joe wasn't listening; he threw the guard off of him and grabbed Joy. She started to scream. She tried to run away from him, the cop said, "Let her go!"

Joe said, "No! Back off or I'll kill her."

"You don't want to do that buddy, put the gun down." Joe didn't know what to do, it was more trouble then he intended. He threw Joy to the ground and kicked her in her back, she screamed. The cop shot at Joe, the bullet went straight into his leg. Joe fell to the ground and was yelling. The guard went back in the hospital to grab some doctors and nurses. They brought in Joy and Joe. Joy was screaming in pain, she knew something was wrong. They took her in the ER and saw that Joy was going into labor; she was only seven months pregnant. They wanted to get this baby out now and Joy was so scared.

"Please don't let my baby die."

"We're going to do everything we can, but you have to relax Joy." The baby was delivered and put into NICU. Joy wanted to see the baby.

Joy's mother was there, she turned to her mother and said, "Mom where's my baby, is he okay?"

"He's fine Joy; they took him into the NICU. You did great honey, he'll be okay, and he's in great hands. You need to sleep now."

"Is Joe gone?"

"There is a guard outside of his room, he's going to be arrested, there are some officers that want to ask you some questions but I told them to come back, you need to rest now sweetie." They decided to talk to Olivia, so they headed up to her room. Olivia was in her bed with her new baby when there was a knock on the door. Her mom answered the door; it was the officers wanting to ask her some questions. Her mom told her about the incident that happened outside with Joy and that man.

"Olivia there is some officers here that want to ask you some questions, do you want to speak to them now or do you want them to come back?"

"No mom, its okay I want to help." Her mom picked up the baby so Olivia could speak to them.

"Olivia this is Detective Schwartz and I'm Detective Harrison. We just want to ask a few questions about Joseph Tyler."

"Sure detectives I want to help."

"When did you last see him Ms. Mallor?"

"The last time I have seen him was when we were held captive at the house a few months ago."

"So you haven't had any contact with him since then?"

"No not at all, he hurt me and he hurt my friend Joy."

"So you're saying that Mr. Taylor is the one that held you two captive for close to a year?"

"Yes detectives, but Chris was the main one, did you find him yet?"

"Unfortunately Ms. Mallor we haven't located Christopher Jensen as of yet."

"Jensen? Don't you mean Duncan?"

"Well Ms. Mallor he had an alias, I don't think he would give his real name, but we are doing everything in our power to find him."

"Is Joy alright?"

"She's fine Ms. Mallor, she did go into labor, she had the baby and they're both doing fine."

"Oh no, It's too soon for her! I hope she's okay. I hope he goes away for a long time for what he did to Joy and me!"

"I wouldn't doubt it Ms. Mallor." "Oh I really hope so."

"That's all the questions for now Ms. Mallor; if we need to get in touch with you we'll call you, or if you need us, just call."

"Thanks detectives." They left the room and Olivia looked at her mom and cried, "Thank God they at least found Joe. I need to see Joy to see if she's okay." Olivia got up and wheeled her baby down to see Joy. Olivia knocked on the door and walked in. "Hey Joy, is everything alright?"

Joy shook her head yes, "Is that you're baby?"

"Yes this is Lea."

"She's beautiful Liv, I'm so happy for you."

"Thanks Joy, and how about you? How are you and the baby doing?"

"We're doing fine, my baby is in NICU though; he needs to cook a little longer," Joy said.

"I'm sure he'll be fine Joy, what did you name him?"

"I named him Ethan Jacob."

"That's such a great name."

"Thanks, can I hold baby Lea?"

"Of course you can." Joy took the baby and held her for a while, "She's beautiful Liv."

She handed the baby back to Olivia and chatted some more, "So they caught Joe. I mean I know he tried to take you again which is awful but I'm glad there was a good outcome. Now we just have to worry about Chris."

"I know," said Joy.

"Hopefully he's far away from here and he'll leave us alone," Olivia said.

"We'll protect our little ones and we have each other to look out for," cried Joy. Olivia and Joy both had smiles on their faces; they thought at that moment that life was perfect. What they didn't know was that Chris was watching their every move. He was not going to leave quietly.

Thirteen

Olivia was released to go home from the hospital the very next day.

She went to visit Joy before she left, "I'll be back to visit okay? I won't leave you hanging."

"Okay Liv, I'll talk to you later and hopefully soon I'll get released." Olivia gathered her baby and left with her mom.

"Mom, I've been wondering where dad has been."

"Well honey, dad is having a hard time dealing with all of this."

"But he hasn't even come to visit me in the hospital, or to see the baby." Olivia cried.

"That's because he didn't think you should have kept this baby, he thinks you're too young to have a child and by a rapist."

"Well it's not his decision to make, the only thing good about this whole situation is my baby and I will never give her up."

"I know Olivia and I told him that but he's just a stubborn man, you know how he can be."

Olivia and her mom finally returned home with baby Lea. When Olivia walked into the living room, her dad looked up at her and smiled.

"I'm glad you're home Liv, I'm sorry I didn't come to the hospital. How are you feeling?" Olivia walked over to her dad and hugged him.

"I'm doing okay dad and I want you to meet someone, this is your granddaughter Lea." Her dad took one look at the baby and his whole face changed, and lit up. Olivia knew that her father had changed his mind about his granddaughter.

"She's beautiful Olivia and she has your eyes."

Olivia had tears in her eyes, "Thanks dad."

Over the past few months, Olivia, her mom, and Joy have been working on the nursery for baby Lea. When Olivia walked in she saw that it was completely finished. The walls were a pretty shade of yellow and there were teddy bear wallpaper lining the whole top of the wall. She walked further into the room and saw a changing table with diapers and all the necessities. The crib was set up with a mobile hanging down. It was perfect.

"Mom and dad thank you so much for doing this for me." Her mom walked over to her and said,

"Your dad finished it Liv; you should thank him for finishing it." Olivia ran into the other room and hugged her dad.

"Thank you so much dad for finishing the nursery, it looks great!"

Her dad hugged her tightly and said, "You're welcome sweetheart."

Olivia walked over to the crib and placed Lea in there, "You'll be safe and sound here Lea," she whispered.

Chris was lurking in the shadows of Olivia's house. It was late and everyone was sleeping in the house. Chris went to the back of the house and tried the back door; he knew that there wasn't an alarm system at the house. The door was locked. He went to the shed and found something to break the lock. He opened the door and it was dark. He took his time going through the house and reached Olivia's bedroom. He opened the door and closed it quietly behind him. He went over to the bed and saw Olivia lying there sleeping; he stood there staring at her for a moment. He put his hand over her mouth and she opened her eyes wide.

"Hey there baby," he whispered. Olivia was freaking out she was so scared. "Shh now, don't make a sound Liv." He got on the bed and pulled her nightgown up, "looking good baby." He grabbed some rope from out of his pocket and tied her hands to the bed.

"Chris, please don't do this," she said loudly.

"I told you to be quiet; he shoved something into her mouth to be quiet. He got on top of her, "This is just like the old days huh Liv?" Tears were streaming down her face. He pulled down his pants and shoved himself inside of her. "Oh baby you feel so good." He knew he had to be quiet and so it lasted longer. Olivia was still sore down there from having the baby. "You deserve this," and he pounded into her. You could hear Olivia whimper, she was in so much pain. He finally reached climax and rolled over on the bed. "Thanks doll, now I want to see my child." She just looked at him and shook her head. "If you don't I will take this knife and jab it into you, then your child won't have a mother. Now you don't want that do you?" Olivia shook her head. "If I take out the rag that's in your mouth, you won't scream will you?" Olivia shook her head no. Chris took out the rag that was in her mouth. Olivia was coughing trying to catch her breath. Chris got up and pulled Olivia up by her hair and she let out a small scream. They heard a door open; it was her parent's door. Chris hid under the bed and dared her to be quiet. Olivia lay back in bed, her mother appeared at the door.

"Are you okay Olivia?"

Olivia looked at her and said, "Yes mom I just had a nightmare, sorry if I woke you."

"It's okay, I thought something was wrong." She stroked Olivia's hair so she could go back to sleep. Olivia pretended she was sleeping and her mom got up and walked out of the room and they could hear their door shut.

Chris got up, "Now be quiet, you don't want anything to happen to your mommy now do you?" Olivia didn't say anything she just got up and walked toward the door. She led him down the hallway and to the right was the nursery. She slowly walked in and there was Lea sleeping. "Well, well, well, isn't she a spitting image of you," he said.

"Chris, please be careful with her, don't hurt her," Olivia cried.

"I wouldn't hurt her Liv, she's my daughter." He looked at Olivia, "We're leaving, grab your things and her things, you're coming with me."

"What do you mean? Where are we going? Please don't do this, I want to stay here."

"Then I'm taking the baby." He started to walk away with the baby and she grabbed him,

"You're not taking her anywhere unless I'm with her."

"That's what I thought now get your shit and let's go." Olivia was so upset and she was shaking, she didn't want to go. She started to walk out of the room but Chris grabbed her, "No way, I'm not leaving you out of my sight; I'm coming with you to your room." Olivia grabbed a few things from Lea's room and Chris followed her into her room to get some things together. "Hurry up," he hissed. Olivia hurried up and they walked back down the hallway towards the kitchen.

"Should I write my parents a note? I don't want them to think it's suspicious that I'm just gone."

"Good idea, just say you needed some time to get away, and you wanted to take the baby with you." Olivia wrote the note and put it on the table. She knew her mom would understand that she would never run away, especially after all that happened.

They left through the back door, Lea was starting to stir, "Shut that baby up!" Olivia hugged

Lea and she was fine. She set the car seat up in his car and put Lea in it and she fell back to sleep again.

Olivia got in the car and asked, "Where are we going?"

Chris looked at her and said, "We're going to get my other baby."

"You can't Chris; the baby is still in the hospital and Joy is too."

"Fuck!" he yelled. "

You have me, you don't need to worry about them," Olivia said. Olivia looked at Chris and his eyes went dark, he was turning again. Chris turned the car on and drove down the street. "Where are we going?" Olivia asked.

"We're going far away from here." Olivia stared out the window, she felt like she was trapped again and she knew that Chris would never take his eyes off of her or Lea again.

*F*ourteen

A few days had passed and Joy was wondering where Olivia was. She hadn't seen or heard from her since she was released from the hospital.

Joy's mom walked in the room, "How ya feeling Joy?"

"I'm doing okay mom."

"Good," said her mom.

"You have a visitor." Joy was so excited that she thought it was Olivia. When the door opened Joy saw that it was Caroline, Olivia's mom.

"Hey Joy," said Caroline. Joy could tell something was wrong.

"What's wrong Mrs. Mallor? Did something happen to Olivia?" Caroline had tears in her eyes.

"Olivia and Lea are gone; she left a note on the kitchen table a few days ago. I think Chris came back for her." Joy's face went white. "I've been in touch with the police so hopefully they find them."

"Oh no, are you serious? I hope they find them both. I can't believe he took her and Lea, he must be out of his mind, the longer they're with him the longer their lives are in danger, who knows what he'll do to them," Joy cried.

Chris and Olivia made it to a hotel one hundred miles outside of town. He got out of the car and stretched. The baby slept the whole way surprisingly. He went around to Olivia's side of the car and opened the door.

"Wake up sleeping beauty, we're here."

Olivia jerked awake and turned to see if Lea was still there, "Oh thank God."

"What, did you think I would take the baby and throw her in the trash?" Chris laughed.

"That's not funny Chris, people do crazy things."

Chris looked at her and grinned, "I want the baby darling."

Olivia pulled Lea out of the car seat, "She needs to be changed, Chris."

"We need to get a room, get the baby and come on. They walked over to the main office and the man behind the desk looked suspiciously at them but didn't say anything, he handed Chris a key and they walked to the room. He opened the door and forced them inside and shut the door. Olivia walked in the room and put Lea down on the bed, she grabbed a diaper and a wipe to clean her. Chris just stood there staring at what she was doing. "Why are you looking at me like that?"

"You're pretty good with the baby," Chris said. "What's her name anyway?"

Olivia looked up, "Her name is Lea." Chris walked over to her and wanted to pick her up but Olivia was hesitant about it.

"Don't look at me like that Liv; I'm not going to break her besides she's my daughter too." Olivia let him pick her up and surprisingly he held her gently. Lea smiled at him. "Hey Lea, I'm your daddy." Olivia had a sad look on her face. "I think she likes me Liv, look at that, she's smiling at me." Chris gave her back to Olivia; she sat down on the bed and pulled up her shirt to feed her. He stood there staring at her.

"Please don't be a perv."

"I can't help myself it's pretty hot." Olivia just shook her head and continued feeding Lea.

"So where are we going after this?"

Chris lay down on the bed, "I told you far away from town. Why don't you put the baby down Liv and come to the bathroom with me."

Olivia looked afraid, "Why?"

"Don't make me say it twice and you should know better to talk back to me!" Olivia took the baby and put her down in the car seat. She walked over to the bathroom. Chris followed her in there and he turned the shower on. "Get in!" Olivia didn't want to, she just stood there. Chris stood over her and pulled her nightgown off; Olivia had tears in her eyes. "Now get in! Don't make me say it again." She got in the shower and Chris took all his clothes off and got in with her. "Doesn't this feel nice?" Chris said. Olivia didn't say anything she just looked down. He pulled her chin up so she could look at him, "I asked you a question."

"Uh yeah," she stammered. Chris just smiled at her and said, "Get down on your knees." Olivia bent down as she was told. "That's my good girl, now I want you to take me in your mouth." Olivia really didn't want to but she knew she had to, for her sake and her daughter's sake. She started sucking him off, and then he pulled her up, he forced her to turn around, and put himself inside her. He was talking dirty and saying obscene things to her. Olivia never said a word she just took it. When he finished, he left her there and went back into the room. She stood there in the hot shower, hoping it would make her numb inside and take her pain away. He yelled into the bathroom, "I'm going to get some shuteye so don't you dare think about leaving this room."

After she showered, she went back to the room and saw Chris was sleeping. Olivia stood there staring at him, she wanted to leave but she was afraid. There was a phone in the room but she knew she would wake up Chris if she tried to use it. Lea was asleep in the car seat. Olivia quietly walked to Chris' side of the bed and saw his keys lying on the floor and he was snoring loudly. She knelt down to pick them up and she got up slowly. She knew she had to get out of there; she didn't want to be a part of his life anymore. She picked up the car seat and Lea started to stir. "Shhh Lea, it's okay." Lea stared at her as if she knew what she was saying. Olivia quietly opened the door to the room and stepped out. She closed the door behind her as quietly as she could. She walked over to the car; she opened the back door and buckled Lea in. She hurried to the front seat and got in. She never drove before. She turned the key and put the car in reverse. The car made a squealing sound, "Shit!" Olivia yelled. The door to the hotel room opened, it was Chris and he was furious. He ran as fast as he could towards the car. Olivia put the car in drive and veered to the left to leave the parking lot. Chris reached for the door handle and it opened, he jumped in and grabbed the wheel. Olivia and now Lea were screaming. Chris smacked Olivia in the face and punched her in her stomach, she couldn't breathe. He was able to crawl to the driver side and stop the car; a couple of people were looking on as they witnessed what was happening. Olivia jumped out of the car and yelled for them to call the police. Chris sped off with Lea still in the backseat.

"No Chris!! Wait!!" She started to run after the car but it was moving too fast. Olivia was screaming and crying, she ran back to the hotel and called the police and then called her parents. "Chris has Lea!!" Olivia told her parents where she was and they came for her as fast as they could. The police arrived on the scene shortly after she called them. It was the same detectives that asked her questions about Chris and Joe.

"Ms. Mallor, could you please tell us what happened?" Olivia was crying again, she was so scared for Lea.

Her mom had her arm around her, "It will be okay Liv they'll find her. Calm down and tell the detectives what happened." Olivia calmed down enough to explain what had happened.

"Chris came into my bedroom a few nights ago; he tied me to the bed and raped me again. He made me take him to Lea's room and then he picked her up and started to take her but I couldn't let her leave without me, so he told me I had to come. That's how we ended up here."

"Would you have any idea where he would be going Ms. Mallor?"

Olivia started crying again, "I have no idea; I just know that he has my baby!"

"We know Ms. Mallor, did you get a check on the license plate, and can you give us the description of the car?"

Olivia had to think a moment, "It's a red 4 door car, I'm not sure of the make. The license plate was FER-9367, I remember because I was running after the car."

"Thanks Ms. Mallor, at least we have that, we will definitely track the vehicle down."

"So what do I do in the mean time?" Olivia said.

"We suggest you go to the hospital to get checked out." Her parents agreed with the Detectives and took her to the hospital. They ended up going to the same hospital that Joy was at since it was the closest hospital. The doctors wanted to make sure that Olivia was okay since she just had a baby. After they checked her they determined that she was doing just fine so she was released. Olivia wanted to visit Joy and tell her what happened. She and her parents took the elevator to the third floor and knocked on Joy's door. Joy was so happy to see her; Olivia ran in and hugged her.

Olivia released Joy and said, "Chris has Lea."

Joy's face dropped and she immediately felt afraid for Olivia and for Lea, "We need to go and find her," said Joy. Just then Olivia's mom's cell phone began to ring, it was the detectives calling.

"Hello," Caroline said.

"Hello Mrs. Mallor, this is Detective Harrison calling, is your daughter with you?"

"Yes detective, she's right here."

"May I speak with her please?" Caroline looked at Olivia, "It's for you Olivia, its Detective Harrison."

Olivia grabbed the phone, "Hello detective, did you find my baby?"

"Ms. Mallor we found the car, we tracked it down to South Carolina. Unfortunately there was nothing in the car and your daughter wasn't in the car either. We are still looking for her; we put out word to the other police stations in the area."

Olivia looked worried; she looked at her mom, "They found the car, but no sign of Chris or Lea." Olivia gave the phone back to Caroline so she could handle the rest of the phone call. Olivia sat on Joy's bed and started to cry.

Joy reached out to her, "It will be alright Liv they'll find her. I know they will."

Olivia looked at Joy and gave a little smile; "I hope so. How is your little one doing?"

"He's a fighter; he's actually doing really well. I'm getting released I think later on today. Ethan has to stay a little longer. I can come and visit him whenever I would like to though. Hopefully he'll be released soon."

"I hope so too," said Olivia. Olivia couldn't help but wonder how Lea was doing and where she was. She missed her more than anything.

*F*ifteen

*E*than was released soon after Joy was discharged from the hospital. Everyday Lea was missing, Olivia was becoming increasingly upset, she didn't want to eat and she even had trouble sleeping. Olivia was starting to get depressed; she didn't really want to be around Joy. After all, Joy had her baby but she knew that Joy was just trying to help.

"You have to eat something Liv; don't you want to be strong for Lea?"

Olivia didn't even look at Joy, "What's the point? They'll never find her."

Joy grabbed Olivia, "They will find her Liv you just have to have faith." Olivia didn't believe in faith, how could she, her daughter was gone. That night Olivia was lying in bed and she was thinking about Lea when she heard a knock on the door.

"Olivia its mom, Joy is on the phone it sounds like something's wrong."

Olivia hurried to the door and opened it; she took the phone from her mom, "Hello."

"Liv, it's Joy, he's gone!" Joy was crying hysterically.

"What do you mean he's gone?" Joy was breathing heavily into the phone.

"Chris took him! He broke in while all of us were sleeping! I had a strange feeling and when I went into Ethan's room he wasn't in his crib. I already called the police and they're on their way over. Liv, could you come here and stay with me."

"Of course Joy, I'll be right there." Olivia hung the phone up and got dressed.

Her mom walked into her room, "Is everything alright?"

"No, Chris took Ethan." Her mom covered her mouth she couldn't believe it. "I have to go over to Joy's, she called the police she needs me.

"Of course sweetie, do you want me to come?"

"No mom, it's okay. Thanks anyway." Olivia made it to Joy's house and saw all the cops there. She knocked on the door and Mrs. Monroe answered.

"Oh good Olivia, get in here, its terrible what is happening with you girls. Joy is out of her mind right now, maybe you can talk some sense into her, she wants to go and find Ethan." Olivia looked at her and felt like something snapped inside her. It was then that she decided that she was going to look for them.

"I'll talk to her Mrs. Monroe." Olivia walked down the hall to Joy's bedroom; she was lying on the bed crying. "Hey Joy." Joy looked up and her face was swollen from all the tears streaming down her face.

"He's only a tiny baby Olivia; he's not going to know what to do with a tiny baby. He needs me."

"I know Joy, they both need us."

Joy turned to Olivia and said, "We need to find them, Liv. The police can't find Chris and he's back in the area, he must have been here the whole time. I don't get it." Olivia looked at Joy and understood exactly how she felt; it was like Chris was toying with them and the police.

"I agree Joy, we need to find them, our parents won't be happy but we have to do what's right for our babies." Joy looked at Olivia and saw a spark of hope. She knew she was right.

"We have to get out of here right now; we can sneak out the window."

"You don't want to tell your mom? She'll be worried sick about you."

Joy looked at Olivia, "She'll make me stay here and wait around for updates and I don't want to do that. I want my baby back now! If it makes you feel any better I'll write my mom a note, and leave it on the bed."

"Okay." Joy wrote a note to her mom explaining that she had to find him and that Olivia was going too. She told her she loved her and will be in contact with her. Joy opened the window and the both of them left in search of their babies.

Olivia and Joy took off in Olivia's car. They drove down the street and turned down the main street. They knew the babies were around here somewhere but not sure where.

"Liv, why don't we try the old house where he kept us before?" Olivia looked at Joy and wasn't sure if that was a good idea.

"Do you think he would be stupid to go back there?"

"Well I don't think we have much choice, we should try it," Joy said. They drove over to Chris' old house. They saw a car on the side of the street; Olivia decided to turn her lights off. She didn't want to look suspicious if Chris was around. She parked the car a little down the street and they started to walk down to the house. It looked abandoned and very quiet. They peaked through the window and didn't see anything.

Olivia whispered, "Do you think we should try the front door?" Joy shook her head and started up the walk to the front door. Olivia went to the front door first. They tried it and it opened. They both looked at each other.

Joy looked at Olivia and said, "Do you think we should really be doing this, I mean without the police."

"We have to, it's for our children." They walked into the living room and didn't see anyone, but they both spotted the diaper bag that was Lea's. "Oh my God Joy its Lea's diaper bag." Olivia walked over to the bag and looked inside. Everything was still there. "They have to be here," said Olivia.

"Come on let's go and get the police."

"Wait Joy, I just want to make sure." They walked through the living room and down the hallway. They walked further down the hall to a bathroom, it was empty, they walked further and there was a bedroom, it was filthy, but still no sign of them. They made their way to the kitchen and on the table and in the sink they saw rotten food and flies were flying all around.

"This is pretty disgusting," Joy whispered.

"If the babies are here, it's really not a good place for them to be," Olivia said. They saw the door that led down to the basement. They looked at the door and then to each other.

"I really don't want to go back down there, Olivia."

"I know you don't, but we need to check." Olivia opened the door, flicked the switch for the light to come on and it didn't work. "Shit," whispered Olivia. "It is way too dark down there, maybe we should look for a flashlight."

"Good idea," Joy said. They walked back into the kitchen and searched for a flashlight, they found one in one of the drawers. Olivia wanted to make sure it worked so she flicked it on, at first nothing but she gave it a few whacks and it turned on. They made their way back down the hallway and into the basement. They started to descend down the stairs and realized they didn't have anything to protect themselves with.

"Liv, maybe we should get a knife from the kitchen."

"Yeah that might be good idea, so they walked back up and into the kitchen again. They opened up the drawers and finally saw a knife that was a little rusty but would do. They walked back down the hallway, opened the basement door and started to go down the steps when they heard a noise.

"Do you hear that," Olivia whispered.

"Do you think they could be down here Liv?"

"That's what we're going to find out." They got to the bottom of the stairs and shined the flashlight around the basement. They saw the window that they broke to get out and it was still broken. To the left they saw the door to the room they were held captive in. That's when they heard another noise, and this time it sounded like a baby whimpering.

"Oh my God, that could be Ethan!" Joy started towards the door and opened it; there on the bed lie the babies, side by side. Joy ran in and picked up the baby, "Oh my God Ethan, I can't believe you're here." Olivia was behind her and saw Lea; she went and scooped her up.

"Joy we have to get out of here. Chris could be here somewhere." They started to walk out when Chris appeared.

"Do you think I'm stupid? Did you think it would be that easy to let you leave?"

"Let us go Chris, please," Olivia pleaded.

Chris looked at her and grinned, "But I missed you Liv."

"No you didn't, you just want our babies and you can't have them!" Olivia tried to push her way to the door but he grabbed her and pushed her back. "Are you nuts? I have Lea in my arms!"

Chris looked at the girls, "I kind of didn't want to do this, well maybe I kind of did, but it looks like you're stuck here again."

"What does that mean?" said Joy.

"It obviously means you're not leaving. Why do you think it was so easy to lure you here?"

"Chris please, don't do this," said Olivia.

"I'm sorry Liv, it's already done."

"But the cops are going to find us here, they know where to look."

"I don't think so, see I made an anonymous tip and said that you were seen outside city limits.

They're not going to look for you here. Oh yeah, by the way, give me your car keys."

"Why?"

"What are you dense, just give them to me!" Olivia just looked at him; she didn't want to give him the keys because then he would have the power. "Is this really how you want to play Liv?"

"Play what? I'm not doing anything." Chris walked over to Olivia and smacked her hard in the face. Lea started to cry and then Ethan started to cry.

"Shut those babies up and give me the damn car keys!" Olivia threw the keys at Chris, "Good girl." He walked out and slammed the door behind him.

Sixteen

They were back where they started, stuck in this room and now with their babies.

Joy started to cry, "I can't be stuck in this room again, Liv. I'll go crazy."

"I know Joy, me too, but we have to stay strong for our babies. We need diapers for them; I don't know what Chris is thinking, how will we survive down here without food?"

"Maybe that's what he wants; maybe he wants to kill us, Oh God!" screamed Joy.

"Joy calm down, that's not what he wants. Why don't you lie down and try to sleep, I'll take care of Ethan for you." Joy decided to lie down and passed out. Olivia decided to try and feed Lea when the door opened and it was Chris, he threw the bags into the room. "Chris we need supplies for the babies, we need diapers and wipes and some formula."

"Jeez Liv, do you think I have everything in the basement down here? By the way that's pretty hot your breast exposed like that feeding her, can I get the other tit," he laughed.

"That's so funny, nothing you haven't seen before, now can you get some for us, please?"

"I'll see what I can do and he left." Olivia felt disgusting and her face hurt where Chris slapped her. She wanted to shower and Lea finally fell asleep. She got undressed and turned the water on. She let the water cascade around her and she melted away. She got out of the shower and went to lay down with Joy and the babies and she fell asleep. Olivia heard the door and jerked awake. "Hello there, cutie pie." He brought in a bunch of bags with supplies and food. "Here is some food for you and Joy and formula for the babies. I also got diapers and all that shit that goes with babies."

"Thanks Chris," Olivia said. Chris walked to the door said you're welcome and left. Olivia dug through the bags and some of this wasn't right, but she had to make it work, what choice did she have? She decided it would be a good idea to change Lea.

Joy woke up and looked up at Olivia, "I thought it was all a dream."

"I wish it were," said Olivia. "Chris brought bags of supplies for us and for the babies."

"At least he did that for us, I have to use the bathroom I'll be right back." Olivia finished changing Lea and wanted to feed her again. Joy came out of the bathroom and looked in the bags. "I guess I should change Ethan, it's been awhile." She changed his diaper and decided to feed him too; she then put him down on the bed. "I hope we're not in here forever and I hope he doesn't do things like he did before," said Joy.

"Well knowing Chris, don't be surprised if he does. Just don't fight it; I don't think he enjoys it as much if you act like you want it." For the next several hours they just sat there thinking how to get out of there once again. They started to get hungry and looked through the bags that Chris gave them; all they found was a little bit of food.

"He thinks we can actually survive on this crap," said Olivia.

Joy looked at her, "I don't think we have a choice." They found some potato chips, some beans, spam, some bread, and bottles of water. Olivia started to eat a bit of food when she ran to the bathroom, when she was done she came out and plopped on the bed.

"Are you okay Liv?"

"I feel okay just a little nauseous."

Joy looked at Olivia, "Maybe you caught a bug." Olivia was thinking and she started to put two and two together.

"I don't think so Joy."

"What do you think it is then?"

Olivia looked at Joy, "Well Chris raped me two times and I think I'm late, my boobs are sore and I feel sick to my stomach. I think I'm pregnant again."

Joy looked surprised, "Are you sure Liv?"

Olivia shook her head, "I need to get Chris to get me a pregnancy test, I'm sure he'll be ecstatic." There was a noise outside the room and they knew that Chris came exactly when they knew he would. He opened the door and brought some chicken in so they could eat a real meal. "Chris I need to ask for something."

"What is it now Liv?"

"I need a pregnancy test."

Chris looked at her and smiled, "Really baby?" She just shook her head. "I'll get on it Liv." He was excited as he left the room.

"I told you he would be excited. He's such a psychopath. I really don't want to go through a whole pregnancy again in this room." Olivia saw that Lea had finally fallen asleep. "Joy do you want me change Ethan?"

"I got it Liv, I should feed him too."

"He looks strong Joy, I'm so happy your baby is okay."

"Me too Liv, he's my little miracle." They put the babies down and decided to relax on the bed.

"You know with everything going on we haven't really discussed what we are going to do after we get out of here," Olivia said. Joy just groaned, I guess we'll figure it out sooner or later.

"At least we're in this situation together. Do you think we'll see each other after this whole ordeal is over?"

"Of course Joy, what makes you think that we won't?"

"I don't know. I know this situation is horrible for the both of us, so maybe you wouldn't want to see me since it's like a reminder."

"But Joy, I have Lea now because of this situation so that doesn't even matter, plus you are my best friend."

"I know Liv, you're mine too."

Seventeen

Olivia and Joy were happy to be together in this situation. They talked about the future, if there was going to be one. They knew they had to finish high school and after graduation they weren't sure and they really hadn't thought about it.

Chris opened the door and walked in, "I got you the pregnancy test and I want to know now if you are pregnant."

"Okay, I have to pee anyway." Olivia got up grabbed the test and Chris followed her, "Are you going to watch the whole time?"

"Yes!" Olivia sat down and took the test out of the packet and peed on the stick, Chris took the test from her and stared at it. Olivia got up and pulled her pants up. Next thing you know he screamed and kissed her. "I knew it baby, another one is coming!"

"I guess that answers that question," Olivia said.

"I got you some vitamins just in case." They walked back into the room and he handed her the vitamins. "After all this excitement, I'm feeling pretty aroused. Joy front and center, it's your turn."

"But Chris, I don't want to have another baby," Joy cried.

"You think I care what you want? Don't talk back to me either, you know what happens." He grabbed her and pulled her clothes off in front of Olivia. Joy was crying hysterically, Olivia tried to pull him off her and he pushed her away. "Really girls, that's how you want to play?" He started hitting Joy in the face and Olivia was screaming for him to stop and the babies were crying. He finally stopped and Joy was just lying there. "You got off this time Joy but that's the last time I'm going to tolerate that. He got up and walked out the door and slammed it behind him.

Olivia ran over to Joy, "Are you okay?" "I think so, just my head hurts."

"I think Chris gave us some pain reliever, I'll get you some." The babies were still crying, Olivia picked up Lea and held her tightly, telling her it was going to be all right. Joy got up off the ground and went to Ethan and hugged him and sang to him. They both finally settled down and they placed them back on the bed. Joy took the pain reliever and lay on the bed. "Joy I told you to do what he says, he's crazy, he could've killed you."

"I know Liv, I just thought maybe he was different this time, he was so happy about you being pregnant again.

"I know Joy, but we have to keep him happy, we don't want to die down here."

Joy agreed and looked at Ethan, "He's my world. I would die if anything happened to him."

"I know I feel the same way about Lea. Let's just get some sleep," said Olivia. She turned off the light and went to sleep. During the night Joy woke up and saw Chris standing there staring at her, he pulled her up and led her into the bathroom.

"I'm sorry baby for doing that earlier, I just got worked up. Do you forgive me?"

Joy looked at him, "Of course I forgive you."

"Okay good, so let's try this again. Lift up your arms." Joy did as she was told. He lifted up her nightgown and just stared at her body, he put his hands all over her. "Turn around." She slowly turned around and he bent her down. She felt him rub against her and slowly put himself inside her. He was gentle at first and then started to pound into her. She was about to scream when he covered her mouth, "Don't scream or I'll hurt you again." Joy just stood there and took it, when it was finished he kissed the back of her head and left. Joy decided to take a hot shower, when she was finished she went back into the room and lay down and cried herself back to sleep.

In the morning, Olivia woke up and went to the bathroom, she walked back into the room and wanted to feed Lea and change her. Joy was still sleeping so she tried not to disturb her. When she was done fixing up Lea she placed her back on the bed. Olivia felt like she was going to vomit and she ran to the bathroom. She hoped that this was going to get easier. When she walked back into the room she saw Joy awake. Olivia walked over to her and said good morning. "I can't get away from this morning sickness. Hey are you alright Joy?"

"He had his way with me last night, in the middle of the night."

"Oh no, that sick bastard, I'm so sorry."

"I took it like you said and he just left. I hate him, I really do Liv."

"I hate him too Joy!" Joy got up and went to the bathroom; she came back and decided to feed Ethan and change him. She put him back down after she was done. "Let's see what other kind of food we have here in this bag." They looked in and decided on Spam.

"Ugh! I could go for a huge stack of pancakes and some sausage," said Joy.

Olivia laughed, "Me too." Chris opened the door when they were just about finished with the Spam.

"Good morning ladies how are we this morning?" Olivia and Joy looked at him and said they were fine. "And how are my babies doing."

"They're good," they said. He walked over to them and kissed them. The girls looked cautiously at one another, making sure he doesn't hurt them.

"I brought you some reading material and puzzles, figured you were bored down here. By the way, I saw on the news that they're out there looking for you girls, oh and Joe was finally taken into custody. Good riddance to him. Alright I'll leave it to you then, see ya later lovers." When Chris left, they pulled out the magazines and the puzzles.

"I wonder if I could stab Chris in the eye with this pen," Joy said.

*E*ighteen

*T*he days were going on and it felt like they were never going to get rescued. Olivia made a chart to know what day it was; she figured they were there for about a month now. The babies were doing well, a little sun deprived but they were healthy. Olivia figured she was about two months along now. She was starting to feel a little better. She worried about Joy; she seemed depressed and tired a lot lately.

"Hey Joy you doing okay today?"

"I'm just kind of tired Liv. I don't really feel like doing much." Chris has been making it a habit of coming in the room in the middle of the night to have his way with her.

"Do you think you could be pregnant?"

"I don't know Liv."

"Well how do you feel besides feeling tired?"

Joy looked at her and said, "Like shit."

"I think maybe you should take a test, next time Chris comes I'll tell him." Joy rolled over. Olivia was holding Lea and snuggling with her, she figured Lea and Ethan to be about 3 months old.

Joy turned to Olivia, "I don't know how you can be so positive being locked down here."

"Well Joy, I really don't have a choice, if I remained upset and mad then I would probably go insane."

"Are you saying I'm insane?"

"Of course not, Joy! I'm just telling you how I deal with it." Joy just lay there saying nothing. Olivia read all the magazines and she was getting tired of the puzzles. "I wonder how long he's been doing this; I mean we can't be the only ones. The bed was already here and there was a built in shower."

"He could've just lived down here and maybe his mom tortured him, maybe that's why he is the way he is." Olivia couldn't take it; she got up and walked around the room, "I feel like there has to be a way out of this room." The whole room had carpet, she figured maybe underneath was just a concrete floor, but she couldn't help but make sure. She started to peel back the layer of carpet, but it was tough. "Joy come on and help me." Joy got up out and walked over to Olivia and knelt down. With the two of them the carpet started to come up. They looked under partially and saw that it wasn't concrete but wood. They wanted to work on it more but were afraid Chris was going to come in any minute, so they pulled the carpet back down. A little bit later Chris showed up, he brought some food and some more diapers. "Oh Chris, we need another pregnancy test."

Chris looked at Joy, "It's about time. I have some upstairs, I'll be right down." He shut the door and a minute later he came back with the test. "Okay Joy, let's go." She followed him into the bathroom, peed on the stick and they waited. And just like last time, he screamed and kissed her forehead, "Another one on the way. I'm feeling proud of myself." They walked back into the room and they told Olivia the news. Joy wasn't happy at all, Olivia tried to smile but she couldn't. "I'll get you some vitamins too Joy."

When he left the room, Joy cried. "I don't want this baby, Liv."

"So what do you want to do Joy, try to miscarry? That's not a good idea and it's not fair. The baby didn't do anything to you, you can't help that Chris is an animal."

"I know Liv, but I hate him, and I really don't want any part of him."

"How could you say that Joy, you have Ethan? You said he was your world."

"I know I'm just upset." Joy realized after Chris found out she was pregnant, he stopped coming around in the middle of the night. Joy thought that it was the only beneficial thing about this situation.

Olivia was concerned about the babies that they weren't getting any sunlight. She was hoping to speak to Chris about something that they could do to help them out with that. When Chris arrived in the morning she asked if she could talk to him.

"What's up baby?"

"I was wondering if we could somehow make like a room or something where we can go outside, supervised of course. The babies need some fresh air and they need sun."

Chris looked at Olivia like she had three heads, "You've got to be kidding with me, right Liv?"

"No I'm not Chris, look at the babies, they look pale, and they need some fresh air. I'm not doing this for us; I'm doing it for them. It's not healthy for them to be locked up in here all day."

He just stared at her for a long time, "Let me think about it."

"Thank you Chris." Chris dropped off more food and supplies. Before he left he turned to Joy, "Are you feeling alright Joy?"

"I'm just tired Chris."

"Okay honey bunny but you do look a little pale. Olivia, follow me to the bathroom," she was worried he was going to rape her again, but when she got inside, he just wanted to talk. "Is she holding up alright?"

"She's just very tired lately; I'm kind of worried about her. I think she needs to see a doctor, but we know how that goes."

"Sorry Liv, you're right you know the rules, you can't leave here. If she seems to get worse, please let me know."

"I will Chris."

They walked out of the bathroom, "I'll see you girls later," and he left.

"What was that all about," Joy said. "He just wanted to make sure you were alright."

"What did you tell him?"

"I just told him you were really tired lately."

"That was all?"

"Yeah that's all."

"Okay."

A few days later Chris came through the door and he looked excited. "So are you ready to see it?"

Olivia said, "See what?"

"I made a special space outside for the babies and for you girls."

Olivia had a huge smile on her face, "You did?"

"Yeah come on." Olivia grabbed Lea and Joy grabbed Ethan and headed upstairs. "Don't think about running away?" He led them up the stairs to the kitchen and out the back yard, and there was a fenced in area so the babies could get some sun. Olivia was so excited, Joy even looked happy, anything to be out of that room. Olivia sat down on the grass and held Lea and she soaked up the sun. She knew it was summer because she'd been tracking the time here. Joy decided to plop down next down to Olivia and held Ethan close.

"What made you decide to do this for us Chris?"

"I'm not that much of a monster." They didn't say anything, they were just happy to be in the warm sun.

Nineteen

Everyday Chris would take the girls and the babies outside and they were grateful. They would lie out under the sun for a few hours until they couldn't take the heat anymore. The babies looked a lot better now that they were getting some sun. Joy's attitude was getting better, she didn't really cry anymore, only sometimes. Olivia was getting bigger and she could only wear the dresses that Chris provided. They've been there for a few months now, Joy and Olivia gave up hope.

"Are you going to keep us here forever, Chris?"

"Liv, that's a great question and the answer, is yes," and he laughed. Olivia just looked at him and she wanted to go back into the room, she was feeling more tired these days.

"I want to go back downstairs."

"Well if you want to go back then everyone has to go back."

Joy looked at Olivia, "I'm ready to go back down too."

"Alright then," Chris said. He took them back downstairs and closed the door.

"Are you feeling alright Liv?"

"Yeah I'm just tired Joy, the way I figure it, I'm probably about five months along now."

Joy looked at Olivia and said, "I guess that means I'm about four months along. I still can't believe he did this to us again. Does he expect us to have these babies here in this room?"

"I think so Joy." Olivia lay down on the bed, "Can you watch Lea for me? I would like to take a nap."

"Of course I will Liv." When Olivia woke up, she heard Joy talking in the bathroom, she wasn't sure if she was talking to Chris or Lea or Ethan. She looked over and saw that the babies weren't around so she got up and went into the bathroom; Joy was giving their babies a bath.

"Is everything okay in here?"

Joy turned around startled, "Jeez Liv, don't sneak up on me like that."

"Sorry Joy, I didn't mean to. So you're giving these two baths huh, they look like they're enjoying it."

"Yea they were laughing and giggling, it was so cute." Just then the door opened and in came Chris, he dropped some food off. Olivia walked into the room and thanked him for the food.

"What are you girls up too?"

"Oh we were giving the babies baths."

"Sounds refreshing," said Chris.

"They seem to enjoy it," said Olivia.

"Liv, how are you feeling?"

"Just tired Chris, I've been napping a lot lately."

"I guess that's normal. How is Joy feeling?"

"She's doing better."

Chris smiled, "Good," and he walked out the door. The girls took their babies and wrapped them up all nice and snug and laid them down on the bed for their naps.

"You know what you need Liv, a nice hot bath."

"That does sound amazing, and Chris won't be around for awhile." Olivia went into the bathroom and started the bath up again. "Do you need any help Liv?"

"Yeah that would be great if you don't mind." Joy helped Olivia get undressed. "My big belly probably makes me look hideous," said Olivia.

"Of course not Liv, you look beautiful. I'm so happy to be here with you," said Joy.

"Me too Joy," Olivia said.

"Oh my God, Chris, we didn't know you were there, it's not what you think."

"Oh really, because it looked like to me that Joy here was about to help you with your bath."

"That's not at all what was happening. I just needed help getting into the tub." They just stared at each other.

"Okay if you say so but now that I'm in here with you both I want to see some action." The girls just looked at each other; they didn't know what to do. "You're going to do what I tell you do, otherwise I'm going to give you both a serious ass whooping." Chris made Joy get undressed and told her to get in the tub with Olivia. She did what she was told. Chris got undressed and joined them. "Liv I want you to kiss Joy."

"Chris please I don't want to do this."

Chris grabbed her face and squeezed it hard. "Do it!" Olivia turned and kissed Joy, Chris put his hands on her chest as she was kissing her. His hand slowly moved down her body and caressed her. "You better moan for me girl." Olivia started moaning. "Liv lean back, Joy I want you to suck her chest." Joy did what she was told to do. Olivia was moaning. "Let's stand up shall we," said Chris. He turned the shower on and water was pouring all over them. "I want you to face each other, but Joy I want you to kneel down and take her in your mouth. Joy did what she was told and Olivia started getting shaky. Just then Chris put himself inside Olivia and was going back and forth inside her while Joy was down there. He didn't want to finish so he pulled out of her and told Olivia to go down on Joy and he went behind Joy and did the same thing.

When it was finished he left the room and slammed the door.

"Thank God that was over," said Joy. "Who knows what's going through his mind. I just want to get out of here.

For the next several days things were a routine with Chris telling them what to do sexually. The girls wanted to be left alone; they didn't want anything to do with him. They were trying to figure a plan for escape again, but this time it seemed hopeless.

*T*wenty

The babies seemed a lot better now that they were getting sunlight. The girls were happy with that but as the months passed it was starting to get a little cooler so they couldn't spend as much time as they wanted to. Olivia was close to her due date, she figured from the calendar she made and Joy was right behind her.

"I really don't feel comfortable with having this baby here, Joy. I'm really scared. What if something goes wrong?"

"You'll be fine Liv, I'm here for you, and we'll be here for each other." Olivia and Joy rested a lot, they both seemed to tire easily now with the both of them being at the end of their pregnancy's and they still had to take care of the little ones.

The next day, Chris came in as usual and gave them their daily food supply. Olivia wasn't really in the mood to eat; she just lay there on the bed.

"You okay Liv?" Chris asked.

"Yes I'm fine, just a little tired." Next thing you know, Olivia was grimacing with pain. "Oh no, my water broke!" Joy looked at Olivia and ran over to her.

"We have to take her to the hospital Chris."

"I told you, you're not going anywhere! You'll have to have the baby here." Olivia was beside herself so she started to cry. "Damn it Chris, we don't know what to do!"

"I'll get some blankets and we'll make her comfortable. Olivia you're going to have to calm down, you can do this baby." They made a spot on the floor, so it would be easier.

"I have to push, it's coming," Olivia screamed. Chris and Joy were ready to get the baby out. Olivia started pushing and the baby was crowning, Olivia was screaming, Joy told her to breath.

"Give one big push Liv." Olivia pushed as hard as she could and the baby came out. Chris took the baby and it was crying.

"Here Joy take the baby." She looked at Olivia and knew she was exhausted.

"I'm going to clean the baby up, I'll be right back." Joy came back and handed Olivia the baby, "It's a boy Liv." Olivia was so happy, and he was a healthy baby. She would name him Elijah Jonathan. "I'm so happy for you Liv and you did so well. How are you feeling?"

"Just a little tired. I guess I should try and get some rest."

"Of course Liv, I'll take care of Elijah for you." Olivia smiled at Joy and gave her baby Elijah a kiss and she went to sleep. The baby was especially good, he hardly cried at all. Chris came in to check on how everyone was doing.

"Hey, how are Liv and the baby?"

"They're both doing very well. Liv is sleeping right now and the baby is lying down, which reminds me, I want to ask if we could get something for the babies to sleep in, like a cradle or something. It's unsafe for all these babies to just be laying down on the bed or in their car seats."

"I'll see what I can do; I mean they are my kids, so I don't want anything to happen to them."Joy just looked at him, she couldn't really think of anything to say to him. Chris walked over to Olivia and stroked her hair and told her she did well He then walked over to baby Elijah, "He looks just like me. Almost time for you too Joy, I can't wait to see what you bring me." Joy just smiled and Chris walked out closing the door behind him. Joy noticed that he didn't look too good; maybe he was stressed out or something. She went back to tend to all the babies. As she was changing diapers, Olivia woke up. Joy heard her groan, "Are you okay Liv?"

"Yeah I'm doing okay, just a little sore. Can you bring me Elijah, I think it's time I try and feed him?" She finished changing diapers and brought over Elijah. Olivia slipped her shirt up and started to feed him, he took right to it.

"I asked Chris to try and get us something for the babies to sleep in, I don't think it's a good idea for them to be lying in the beds and in their car seats," Joy said.

"Good thinking."

"You know Liv, I was looking at Chris and he didn't look too good."

"You know, that's funny that you mentioned that because I noticed he wasn't looking too well either when he was here earlier when my water broke. Maybe he was squeamish about it," she laughed.

A few days later, Chris popped in and the girls could tell there was something wrong with him. His color was off and he was coughing a lot.

"Here I brought you some cradles for the babies to sleep in. How are all my babies doing?"

Olivia looked at him, "Everyone is doing great. How are you doing? You don't look or sound very well, that cough worries me."

He looked at her with a strange grin, "Don't think you can get rid of me."

"I wasn't thinking that at all, I'm just concerned."

"Well I'm fine, I'll be back later to give you some supplies," and he left.

"I don't like the way he looks or sounds," said Joy. "What if he's contagious and the babies or us could get it?"

"You're right Joy; we'll just have to keep the babies away from him." A few hours later, Chris brought the supplies, extra diapers and some food. He looked even worse.

Olivia said to him, "Chris I think you should go and lay down, you don't look so hot."

"Thanks Liv, you really know how to make a guy feel good." He left the room and went upstairs and crashed on the couch. The girls were pleased with the cradles and they felt the babies would be a lot safer now. They now could sleep comfortable in the bed. Elijah woke up the girls by crying. Olivia walked over to him and felt his diaper and it was a mess. She cleaned him up and she fed him and he finally settled down.

The next morning, the girls woke up and the babies were stirring. Olivia went to Lea and picked her up. She changed her diaper, fed her, and put her back down. Joy went to Ethan as he was awake as well so she did the same. After all the babies were situated, Olivia decided to take a shower. When she got out Chris was in the room, bringing breakfast and checking on things. He was hacking away.

"Are you sure you're all right Chris?" asked Joy. He mumbled something and he left the room. Olivia came out of the bathroom and Joy said to her, "He didn't even want to chat, something is definitely wrong. Not that I'm complaining."

"I know what you mean Joy, but oh well we can't do anything but keep our babies safe from him.

*T*wenty-one

A few weeks have passed and it seemed like Chris was coming less and less. Joy was starting to get more uncomfortable; she knew it was almost time to have her baby. The babies were all settled in with their cribs. Olivia and Joy decided to play some cards when Chris came in and he looked terrible. He grabbed Olivia and forced her into the bathroom, told her to get undressed. He wanted his way with her. Olivia decided she wasn't going to listen to him, she thought he seemed weak so when they got to the bathroom she acted like she was going to undress. Instead, she turned around and shoved him and he fell backward. When he fell he hit his head. He was furious, he tried to swing at Olivia but he missed. It was like he was drunk, but Olivia thought it was the illness, whatever was wrong with him. Chris got frustrated and left the room and slammed the door behind him. All the babies started crying and Joy and Olivia had to work to try and keep them calm and stop crying.

Joy looked at Olivia, "What was that all about?"

"He wanted to have his way with me and I had enough so I pushed him and he fell and hit his head. He tried to hit me but he missed, I guess he got frustrated and left."

The next day they went back to their card game but then Joy's water broke.

"Oh jeez, it's time." Olivia did the same thing for Joy as she did for her, got her comfortable and prepped for her to have her baby. Joy had a C-section so this time was going to be different for her, but she was prepared. Joy was ready to push and Olivia was there to catch the baby. Olivia saw the baby was crowning.

"Just one more push Joy," she pushed and out came the baby. Olivia took the baby and cleaned her up. Olivia walked over to her and smiled, "It's a girl," and she handed her the baby. "Have you decided what you're going to name her?"

"I decided on Hope Anne."

"That's a beautiful name." Joy smiled at her and then looked at the baby. "Do you want to rest up Joy? I can look after the baby for awhile." Joyce gladly obliged. Olivia was taking care of the baby when she realized that Chris hadn't come today. She was thinking Chris was mad at her for pushing him.

She was resting with the babies when Joy woke up, "Hey, how are the babies?"

"They're doing good Joy, they're all sleeping. So I'm kind of worried because Chris hasn't come today with food, I hope I didn't make him mad."

"I'm sure he's fine, maybe he's just late today."

"Hopefully," Olivia said. They went back to their normal routine of what they do daily, they read books, cleaned up, ate a little bit, changed diapers and fed the babies. It seemed like hours went by and still no word from Chris. The girls were starting to get worried.

"What if something happened to him?" asked Joy.

Olivia thought about it, "I know he's been sick, maybe he got worse." They decided to lie down and call it a night. When they woke up, they did their morning routine and waited for Chris but he never showed up. "Now I know something's wrong, he would've been down here by now, mad or not, he wouldn't let us starve." Olivia was worried because if Chris weren't around, then they would definitely be trapped down there. "We have to figure a way out of here Joy. I don't think Chris is coming back."

"How are we going to do that Liv? We tried that before, there is nothing in this room."

"Well we have to try." So they searched around the room, trying to find anything that could work. The door to get out was a plain wooden door with a knob that locked and the outside had a latch on it as well. The girls tried to kick the door open but no luck. There was a thump and then they heard someone coming down the steps, Chris unlocked the door and the latch and walked in. He looked awful.

"What was that noise?"

"What noise, there wasn't any noise."

Chris looked at the girls and the babies, "I swear I heard a noise." Chris was swaying back and forth and his eyes were beat red. He could barely stand up straight. Joyce looked at Olivia and she grabbed the lamp that was on the floor and smashed it over his head. Chris fell to the floor.

The girls looked at each other, "Oh my God Liv, I can't believe you did that."

"Well it was now or never. I had to do what was best for us." They wrapped the babies up as best as they could and they walked hurriedly up the stairs. They walked down the hallway and wanted to search for Chris' keys to his car. They went from room to room and there was no luck.

"They might be in his pocket Liv."

"Okay, I'll go back down and find them." She ran down the stairs and looked in the room and saw that Chris was still lying on the ground. She started going through his pockets, that was when Chris reached for her wrist and he pulled her down.

She screamed and he told her, "You're never leaving me."

"Get off of me!!" And she kicked him in the face. Chris blocked her from hitting him and grabbed her leg, and punched her in the stomach and she fell over clutching her stomach. Chris got up and walked towards the door and slammed it shut so she couldn't get out.

He walked up the stairs and saw Joy with the babies; he snuck up to her and said, "Where do you think you're going?" She started to scream and he put his hand over her mouth, she tried to bite him but she didn't succeed. "You bitches do nothing but cause me problems!" He grabbed the babies from Joy and pushed Joy down the stairs and she landed with a thud. He took the babies one by one and down into the basement and put them in the room. Olivia was still lying on the ground holding her stomach. Joy was laying on the basement floor out cold. Chris picked her up and put her on the bed in the room; he shut the door and locked it. They missed their chance to escape.

*T*wenty-two

*T*he next morning, Olivia and Joy were really sore from Chris hurting them. They tried to manage and do what they normally do when they woke up. They changed, bathed, played, and fed the babies. Chris came down with food and he noticed the girls were huddled together with their babies.

"I'm not going to do anything." He put the food down and he left the room. They rummaged through the food and ate.

"He seems better today, I thought he was deathly ill," said Joy.

"Yeah me too, I have no idea." After they were done eating, they sat there and started to cry, they thought that they were going to get out of there.

"What are we going to do Liv?"

Olivia looked at her, "We have to be strong, if not for each other than for our babies. They need us."

"Yeah I know but it's so hard." Olivia put her arm around Joy and hugged her tightly. The days were dragging on and on; Chris would slip in and slip out. They weren't sure how long they were down there, Olivia started to lose track of time. Lea and Ethan were growing so fast; they were both starting to crawl. The other two babies were doing okay which they were happy about but they were discouraged because they couldn't get sunlight, Chris wasn't allowing them to go outside again. They were feeding the babies when the door opens and he pushed a girl in. The girl looked to be about sixteen, her hair was a mess and she had tears streaming down her face.

Olivia looked at Joy, "Oh no not another girl." Olivia got up and walked over to the girl. "Hey are you okay?" She looked at Olivia stunned; she didn't realize that there would be someone else in here.

"Who are you?" she asked.

"My name is Olivia and this is Joy and these are our babies, Lea, Ethan, Hope Anne, and Elijah."

"What are you doing down here? How long have you been here? What is going on?" She started to cry and breathe heavily.

"Hey come here and sit down. Try and calm down. We've been here for a while now it feels like. I've lost count and this is the second time we've been down here. We escaped before but he found us, more like he took our babies and we came back. He raped us numerous times and we had his children. Joy and I had two of them at the hospital but the other two were born here." The girl looked like she was going to freak out; Olivia put her arm around her. "What's your name?" Olivia could barely understand what she was saying because she was crying so hard, but she made out Sarah. "Okay Sarah, you need to calm down, can you tell me what happened?" The girl started to calm down, and started talking.

"I met Chris at the fair a few months ago; I thought he was this amazing person. We started dating and we were always together, and then this happened." Tears started to form again.

"It's okay, we're here for each other," said Joy.

"Is he a monster? Why would he rape you?"

Olivia looked at her, "We think he wants to have as many kids as possible. I think he has a mental disorder. Can I ask you something?"

"Sure."

"Are you a virgin?"

"Yeah but what does that have to do with anything?"

"Just be aware that he will come for you eventually." The girl looked scared and was mumbling that she didn't want to be there. "We'll try and protect you as much as we can, but he's strong and very persistent."

She looked at Olivia and asked her, "How come both of you are in here?"

"Well he got to me first, I fell for his stupid tricks and thought I was in love with him. We slept together and I was a virgin. After that he put me in here."

"Is that what happened to you Joy?"

"Yeah basically the same kind of thing, it's strange that you're still a virgin and he didn't get to you yet, I thought that was his MO."

"So these are all your babies and they're all from him?"

"Yes these are our children."

"I can't believe this is happening to me," said Sarah.

"Trust us; we understand where you're coming from. Hopefully we can be strong enough to take him down eventually," said Olivia.

The next few days Chris came in to drop off food and supplies and then he would leave. He wouldn't really say anything to them. The girls were starting to get worried.

The next day Chris came in with some rope. First he walked over to Joy and told her to put her hands behind her back. She started to cry and asked him what was happening but he didn't say anything.

He pulled her arms back and tied her up. Then he went to Olivia, she was pleading with him to stop when he smacked her upside the head and the room starting spinning. He took her hands and tied them back. He placed Joy and Olivia side by side. Then he walked over to Sarah and she was crying. He grabbed her and threw her down on the bed. She started kicking and screaming. Chris had some duck tape in his pocket. He held her down and pulled it out and put it over her face.

"No screaming Sarah, be a good little girl." Olivia and Joy started to scream and he looked at them, "Don't you dare ladies, you know what happens when you misbehave." They sat there quietly and Chris grabbed more of the rope and tied Sarah to the bed. He decided the last minute he would duck tape Olivia and Joy's mouths as well. He went back to Sarah, he lifted up her shirt, and he stared at her. "You look beautiful Sarah, I can't wait to explore you." She was crying so hard but the tape held her mouth shut. He ripped her bra off to where she was exposed. "Your chest is amazing baby. I always pictured myself sucking on them." He bent down and started to kiss her chest. Sarah was moving around like a fish, "I would keep still if I were you." She realized that he would hit her, so she just lay there. He started to unbutton her pants and pull off her jeans. The way the girls were positioned he wanted them to watch, like some sick perverted fantasy. They kept turning their heads so they wouldn't see. He pulled down her underwear and tossed it aside. He pulled her legs apart, "Very nice." He put a finger inside her and she winced, "Oh yea nice and tight for me." He got up and pulled his pants down; he got on top of her and forced his way inside. She was screaming in fear and in pain. He moved faster and faster and didn't care if it hurt her or not. When he was finished he got off her and untied her. She was crying and pulled her legs up to her chin. "You may want to untie your new friends." He opened the door and left. Sarah got up and went to Olivia and Joy and untied them and took off the tape. They wrapped their arms around each other and held each other.

"There's a shower over there if you want to clean yourself up."

"I don't understand how someone can be so mean and be a monster; he seemed like the sweetest guy."

"We felt the same way as you did," Olivia said. Sarah got up and went to the shower; her life would never be the same again.

*T*wenty-three

They woke up the next day and Olivia and Joy went about their normal routine.

"Do you guys need any help?"

"Sure if you could help change the babies that would be great," said Olivia. Sarah got right to it.

"How does a normal day usually go?"

Olivia looked up at her, "Well Chris usually comes in and gives us food and supplies and then we eat. We take care of the babies and we just do whatever we can with what we have down here. Sometimes we read, sometimes we play cards, we play games, and sometimes we just talk about life."

"I hope I can stand it," said Sarah.

Joy looked up at her, "In all honesty we don't really have a choice." Just then the door opened and in came Chris with the food and supplies; Sarah was scared so she went as far as she could from him.

"How are my ladies doing this morning?"

Olivia turned to him, "Just wonderful."

"That's good to hear, and where is my new flower? Ah there she is." He walked over to her, "How are you feeling babe?" She didn't say anything but she looked scared to death. "I'm not going to hurt you Sarah."

"You hurt me last night."

"Did I really hurt you? I'm sorry about that. Please come with me," and he put his hand out. Sarah hesitated at first but then she took it and he pulled her up, he hugged her tightly. "I'm going to take care of you, let's go into the shower."

"But I already took a shower," she looked at Olivia and Joy.

"You might want to listen to what the others say; they know how I can get. I would do what you're told." Chris started to pull her to the shower when she started to cry. Chris was getting impatient. He pushed her into the bathroom and closed the door. "You have to listen to me Sarah, you're not going to get away from me, you're all mine now." He started rubbing his hands all over her body. He turned the water on and as he did that she started to go to the door. He pulled her back and hit her in the face. She held her face and was crying.

"Please don't do this."

"I'm sorry baby but it's already done. Now get undressed." She did as she was told and tried to cover herself up but he pulled her arms down. "Don't be shy now; you have nothing to be ashamed of." He told her to get in to the shower and she listened. He took off his clothes and got in the shower with her. He rubbed his hands all over her body and grabbed the sponge. He lathered some soap and he started to wash her thoroughly. He told her to turn around and she obeyed. He grabbed her chest from behind and then he went down below and stroked her. "You better act like you want it, tell me you want it."

"I want it."

"That's my good girl." He pulled her arms against the wall and he forced himself inside her. "Oh baby you're so tight, you feel so good." He went deeper inside her and moved faster. He grabbed her hair and pushed her head back. She started to scream, "I told you not to scream!" He pushed her forward and she smacked her head on the wall. She started to feel a little dizzy and started to fall down. "I'm not done with you yet sweetie." He picked her up and went out of the room; he threw her down on the bed.

Olivia and Joy just looked at him, "What are you doing Chris?"

"Mind your own business; I'm not done with her yet." He stormed over to the girls and pushed them into the bathroom and shut the door. He made his way back to Sarah. She was slightly knocked out but that didn't stop him. He turned her over and pushed himself inside her again. He started to move quickly and that's when Sarah jerked awake. She looked up at him and tried to scream. He grabbed her throat and squeezed, she couldn't breathe. He finally finished inside of her and let go of her throat. She rolled over and coughed. "Don't ever fight me because you will lose!" He got up and grabbed his clothes and left the room. Sarah started to cry and Olivia and Joy ran over to her and covered her up.

"Are you okay?" asked Olivia.

"No, I'm not okay, this is not okay!" She was crying hysterically, "I just want to be left alone."

"Okay but if you need anything we'll be here." Olivia and Joy went back to what they were doing. They played with the babies and fed them and changed them. They were playing cards when Sarah sat down next to them. Her face was so red from all the tears and being upset. "Are you feeling any better?" Olivia asked.

"I guess."

"Just know that he's never going to stop, he's insane. I'm really sorry that you have to go through this but at least you have us here with you."

"I thought he was the person I was meant to be with. I can't believe this is happening. It feels like I went from a fairytale to a nightmare."

"That's how Joy and I felt."

"Can I play cards with you?"

"Of course," said Joy. They dealt her cards and they played. "Why don't you tell us a little about yourself Sarah, maybe it will help to get him off your mind?"

"Okay well I'm sixteen and I'm from Arden. I have a brother and sister. My brother is James, he's twenty-two. My sister is Kim and she's eleven. I'm a tenth grader at River Hills."

"What do you do for fun?"

"I like to play softball, read, listen to music, watch movies, hang out with my friends, and being with my family."

"Sounds a lot like what we like," said Olivia.

Sarah looked sad again, "Those were the things that I enjoyed."

"Don't worry, we'll get out of here, I promise."

"I really don't want to get pregnant; I'm scared to death about that whole thing."

"We felt the same way," said Joy.

"Where are the both of you from?" Olivia spoke up first, "We both actually live in Ashville. I'm eighteen now and Joy is seventeen."

"How long have you been down here?"

"We were down here the first time for I'd say about year. This time it's been months. We kind of lost track exactly how long it's been."

"How old are your babies?"

"Lea and Ethan are both about a year and Elijah and Hope Anne are a few months."

"They're beautiful babies; I can't believe you gave birth to them here in this house."

Joy and Olivia looked at each other, "Fortunately we both had Lea and Ethan at the hospital, but the other two we had here and we couldn't have done it without each other."

*T*wenty-four

As the days went on, the girls decided it would be better to remain low key. When Chris came in they tried not to talk to him, but as usual he took advantage of Sarah and had his way with her. Every day it was the same thing; he barely touched Olivia and Joy. Sarah was starting to go numb inside. Olivia and Joy were worried about her. They tried to get her to eat but she didn't want to. All she wanted to do was sleep and that resulted in her getting weak.

The next day when Chris came in, Olivia decided to talk to him about Sarah. She pulled him aside.

"I need to talk to you."

"Okay, what's up?" She pulled him into the bathroom and shut the door.

"There is something wrong with Sarah. She's not eating and all she does is sleep."

"What do you want me to do about it?"

"I think you should take it easy on her."

"Is that right, what are you going to do for me?"

She looked at him cautiously, "Seriously Chris?" He looked at her and shook his head. "What do you want?"

"Get down on your knees."

"You're going to take it easy on her if I do this?"

"Uh huh, I will." She didn't want to but she felt like it was necessary, she got down on her knees and did what she thought was right. It didn't take him long. He walked out of the bathroom and walked up to Sarah. He picked her up and carried her out of the room. Olivia and Joy were surprised. "What the hell." Olivia said.

"He never did that before," said Joy. They both put their ear to the door and they didn't hear anything. "I hope she's okay." They waited for Sarah to come back but she didn't return. It felt like hours went by and still nothing. The girls tended to their babies and took care of them; they read to them and coddled them. When they put the babies down for sleep they crawled into bed themselves. They lay there looking up at the ceiling, hoping they get out of there so they can put this all behind them.

The next day they woke up and went about their business. The door opened and in came Chris without Sarah.

Olivia went up to him, "Where is she?"

"She's fine."

"How come she's not here? Where is she?"

"I told you Liv, she's fine, she's upstairs."

"How come she can go up but we can't? We have children down here, your children?"

He walked up to her and got in her face, "Who do you think you're talking to like that?" He grabbed her hair and pulled her down. Joy ran over and tried to stop him but he pushed her off of him and she fell back and hit the wall. He pushed Olivia's head into the floor and she screamed. She tried to claw at him but she was unsuccessful. He pulled her up and took the rope from his back pocket and tied her up, "If you're not going to listen to me then this is for your own good." He ripped her clothes off and threw her down on the bed. First he got on top of her and pushed himself inside her. He then flipped her over and wedged his way into her behind; she started screaming and crying. "Don't ever ask me questions like that again and think you can talk to me however you want to!" He finished with her and got up and walked out of the room. Olivia lay there on the bed in pain and she was crying. Joy was on the floor unconscious.

When Olivia felt like she could move, she got up and went to Joy.

"Joy, are you okay, Joy, wake up."

Joy finally opened her eyes, "What happened?"

"Chris came in and he pushed you off of me. I think you fell and hit your head." Joy looked at Olivia and knew something bad happened.

"Are you okay Liv?"

"He hurt me pretty bad this time. He got me in my behind and it hurt like hell."

Joy got up, "I'll turn the bath on for you, I'm sure it will make you feel better." Olivia made sure the babies were okay and they were fine. Olivia got up and walked to the bathroom, "It's ready for you."

"Don't leave me Joy; I don't want to be alone."

"Liv I really don't feel comfortable leaving the children alone but I'll be right out here if you need me."

"Okay thanks Joy." When Olivia finished she got up out of the tub and got dressed, she walked out of the room to see her babies and said to Joy, "Do you think Sarah is still up there?"

"I honestly don't know." The babies were awake so they decided to feed, change, and play with them. Lea and Ethan were starting to stand up and Olivia and Joy were amazed. "Oh my God, they're going to start walking." The girls watched and helped them as they both took their first steps. The day started off horrible but ended very well. Both girls had a smile on their faces.

*T*wenty-five

*T*he next day Sarah came in and this time she brought the food and supplies.

"Oh my God Sarah, are you okay?" She looked at them with a hateful face.

"Please don't speak to me; here is your food and supplies."

"What do you mean don't talk to you, what the hell is going on? Olivia said.

"Chris is taking good care of me; we're going to be together. You guys are just jealous and you hated me from the moment I came here. Chris wants to be with me and wants us to get married; he's just hanging on to you because of the kids."

"What are you talking about Sarah, he's brainwashed you!"

"He said you would say that Olivia, but no, you're the brainwashed ones. I have to go, here is your food and supplies. Have a lovely day." She opened the door and locked it behind her.

"Okay what the hell was that about, what happened to her?" Joy looked at Olivia, "Is she nuts or what?"

"She's only sixteen Joy; he probably would've put anything in her head."

"What are we going to do now?"

"I guess we'll have to figure out something."

Meanwhile upstairs, Sarah walked back into the living room, "Is everything alright down there?"

"Everything is fine Chris. I still don't see why we have to keep them around. Why don't we get rid of them and keep the kids?"

"Well for starters, if you haven't noticed they are fighters. They would stop at nothing to fight for their lives as well as their kid's lives."

"Then maybe we should you know, get rid of them."

"Okay Sarah we will not be doing that, but that's a pretty good suggestion." He leaned over to kiss her. He picked her up and took her to his bedroom. Olivia and Joy couldn't believe that Sarah fell into Chris' trap.

"I can't believe she turned just like that, she's only been gone a few days. I wonder what he said to her," said Joy.

"I'm sure whatever he said to her, he made her feel wanted." Olivia and Joy went about their business and took care of their kids. Lea and Ethan were now walking so they had to be careful that they didn't pick up things and eat them. All they had were each other and their babies. They needed to figure out a plan to get out of there. Who knows what they, Chris and Sarah were capable of.

The next morning they woke up and Sarah was in the room staring at them.

"Jeez Sarah you scared the crap out of me, what are you doing here?"

"I came to pay a visit to see how everyone is doing."

"We're doing fine," said Olivia. Sarah walked over to the babies and leaned over the crib of Hope Anne. She reached down and picked her up.

"Sarah what are you doing?" Joy looked worried.

Sarah looked at her and smiled, "Don't worry Joy, I won't do anything crazy." Sarah put the baby back down into the crib.

"What has he done to you Sarah?"

"He hasn't done anything to me, I love him, and he loves me. He just opened my eyes."

"Opened your eyes to what, to keep us hostage and to hurt us anytime he feels like?"

"Of course not, but he made me see what real love is."

"Don't be silly Sarah you're only a kid. Don't you see he's brain washing you?"

"You're just jealous Olivia." Olivia was starting to get irritated; she couldn't understand why Sarah was falling into his trap. She walked over to her and slapped her in the face. "What the hell Liv!"

Olivia took a step back, she realized what she did was wrong, "I'm so sorry Sarah; I don't know what came over me."

"You're going to be sorry that you did that." Sarah turned and left the room and closed the door behind her.

"What did you do that for?" Joy asked.

"She just got under my skin. We can take her Joy; we have to get out of here. I'm worried they're going to do something to us or one of our babies."

"Liv, I don't know how you would like us to do that. Don't forget about how Chris is, he's just as crazy and who knows what he'll do." The girls sat there quietly and tried to think of something but they couldn't think of a thing. They decided to call it a night and went to sleep.

During the night, the door opened but the girls didn't hear anything. Sarah walked in and stared at them in bed. For a split second she envied them. She turned away from them and went to the cribs of the babies and picked up Elijah, Olivia's youngest. She walked out of the room and closed the door behind her.

When Olivia woke up, she went to the bathroom and then she went about her routine to feed the babies. She went over to the crib and saw that Elijah was gone.

She screamed and cried out, "Where is my baby!"

Joy heard her and woke up, "Liv what's wrong?"

"Elijah, he's gone. He's not in his crib. I know she has something to do with this. I'm so going to get that bitch." When the door opened, in came Sarah.

"Good morning girls."

"Where is my baby?"

Sarah looked at her and smiled, "I don't know what you're talking about Liv."

"The hell you don't. I know you came in here in the middle of the night and took him."

"Now why would I do something like that?"

Olivia could sense the sarcasm, "You know damn well why."

"Oh right how could I forget? I think it was something to do with you slapping me yesterday."

"I want my baby back and I want him back now!"

"I'm sorry I really don't know what you're talking about." Olivia snapped, she walked over to Sarah and threw her against the wall and started hitting her. Joy tried to get her off of her but Olivia was too strong. Sarah was now lying on the ground and her face was mangled. Olivia grabbed the rope and tied her up.

"We're getting the hell out of here and fast, but first we have to take care of Chris."

"How are we supposed to do that?" asked Joy.

"I'm going upstairs." Before Joy could say anything more Olivia ran out of the room and up the stairs. When she made it to the stop step she became really quiet and tiptoed. When she didn't hear anything; she slowly made her way around the

161

kitchen. She grabbed a knife from the drawer and continued on out of the kitchen and down the hallway. She peered into the living room and saw Elijah on the couch. He was wrapped in a blanket and appeared to be all right. She didn't want to take any chances going to him with Chris around. Olivia started walking down the hallway and looked in each room.

She heard Chris yell out, "Is everything alright down there babe?"

Olivia knew she had to say something; otherwise he would come out and check, "uh huh."

"Then get your sweet cheeks in here then." Olivia started to follow the voice; she had the knife in her hand ready to do what she had to do. She walked inside and Chris was lying on the bed facing away from her.

"Hiya lover," was all she could muster as she plunged the knife down into his back. He screamed and got up; Olivia didn't know what to do so she started to run.

He caught up to her and smashed her into the wall, "You fucking bitch, what the hell were you thinking!" he yelled. She fell back and gasped and then he kicked her in the gut. She became breathless and fell on the floor. When he turned around she looked up and saw the knife. She reached up and grabbed it. "I don't think so!" He reached for her but she stabbed him in his hand and he screamed. Just then Joy appeared and kicked Chris right in the back and he fell forward. Olivia took the knife and stabbed him again in his side. He was breathless, lying on the floor. Joy walked over to Olivia and helped her up.

"Are you okay?"

"Yeah I think so, let's get out of here." Olivia walked down the hallway and grabbed Elijah and walked him back downstairs. When she entered the room, Sarah was still tied up. "I'm sorry Sarah, but you're boyfriend is unconscious and he won't be able to hear you or help you."

"What did you do to him?"

"I didn't kill him if that's what you think. He deserves it but I didn't. Instead he will suffer for a while. Good luck with everything."

Olivia and Joy packed up their stuff and went back upstairs to look for the car keys. Olivia walked into the bedroom where she thought they were and Chris was still lying there. She found the keys on the end table. She picked them up and walked out of the door and into the hallway.

"I'll get you for this," Chris said.

"In your dreams asshole," and she kicked him in the stomach. Olivia met Joy at the front door and they walked out to the car. They loaded everything in and started the car. They drove as fast as they could to the police station.

*T*wenty-six

*O*livia and Joy went to the police station first before anywhere else. They wanted to talk to the detectives they spoke to before. They pulled up and gathered the babies and went inside.

"We need to talk to Detective Harrison or Detective Schwartz."

The woman at the front desk looked up and said, "Your name please."

"My name is Olivia Mallor and this is Joyce Monroe, please this is an emergency."

The woman recognized the names, "I know who you both are we've been searching all over for you! I'll be right back." The girls took a seat and waited for the detectives. When they came over they looked shocked.

"Ms. Mallor, Ms. Monroe, please follow us." They followed the detectives into the interview room.

"We were able to get out and we came straight here." The detectives couldn't believe it.

"Where is Mr. Jensen?"

"He's at the house where we were held hostage before. I managed to stab him a few times before we got out of there. He also kidnapped another girl but then became an accomplice alongside him. I tied her up in the room where we were held in the basement."

"You both were being held there again? We didn't even think to look there, I'm so sorry," said Detective Harrison. Olivia put a hand on his shoulder and told him it was fine.

"We would really like to call our parents if you don't mind."

"Of course there is a phone over there, take your time. We should get you girls and your children to the hospital as soon as you're done." When they finished making their phone calls, they got in the car and drove themselves and their children to the hospital.

When they arrived at the hospital, Olivia's parents were waiting for her and Joy's mother was waiting for Joy. When Olivia's parents entered the hospital room, they hugged her and cried.

"We thought we would never see you or Lea ever again, are you okay, is she okay?"

"Yes mom we are both great, but I have something to tell you."

"What is it sweetheart?"

"Well I had another baby, a boy, Elijah Jonathan." Her mom looked surprised.

"But you had Lea about a year ago. How could you possibly?"

"I got pregnant right away when Chris raped me before he took me. He raped Joy too and she had another baby too, a girl, Hope Anne. Everyone is doing okay."

"I have to see this beautiful boy, I'll be right back."

167

Olivia's dad stayed with her, "I hope you're not mad at me dad."

He came over to her and hugged her, "I could never be mad at you Liv. I'm so happy to have you back."

"What about the other baby? I know you weren't happy about Lea."

"Are you kidding I love Lea and I'll love this one too. If they're a part of you, I'll always love them."

"Oh daddy," Olivia cried. Olivia's mom came in and following her was the nurse and she wheeled in Elijah. The nurse picked him up and handed him to Olivia. Olivia's mom was holding Lea and she was smiling.

"Both of your children are doing well. You took great care of them. We do need to check you out though so we would like to take you down to ultrasound."

"Okay no problem. Mom can you watch them for me?"

"We'd love too. Your father and I will watch over them and we'll be right here when you get back." They wheeled Olivia down to radiology to get the ultrasound. She was waiting when she saw the news report of Joy, Chris, Sarah, and herself. She just wanted to block it out.

"I'm so sorry about that, I'll shut it off."

Olivia looked up, "It's okay." "My name is Larissa; I'll be doing your ultrasound today." She took Olivia into the room and performed the ultrasound, "You know you're a very brave and strong girl."

Olivia looked at her and smiled, "I had to be for my children." When the ultrasound was over she was wheeled back to her room. Olivia looked back at the woman, "Thank you Larissa."

"You're welcome honey." When Olivia returned to her room, her mom and dad were holding the babies.

Her mom looked up, "You've done well sweetheart." The doctor came in and told her that everything was fine and that she could go home tomorrow. They just wanted one more day to monitor her and the babies.

"That's fine doctor, thank you." Just then the detectives came in and wanted to speak with Olivia.

"Hello Ms. Mallor, how are you feeling?"

"I'm doing okay detectives."

"We just wanted to talk to you about what happened. We already spoke to Joy and now we just want a statement from you. Do you mind?" Olivia realized she hadn't spoken to Joy since she's been here.

She looked over at her parents, "Have you seen Joy?"

"I didn't get a chance to talk to her but I did speak with her mother. She told me they were all doing fine."

Olivia looked relieved, "I'll have to visit her soon."

"Can you talk to us about what happened?" Olivia looked like she didn't really want to talk to them about the events that took place but she knew they only wanted to help.

"Okay I'll try."

"Honey if you don't want to tell them right now maybe they can come back?"

"No mom it's okay. When Chris took Lea, there was nothing I could do except wait until I heard something. That's when Joy called me and told me that Ethan was taken. I just snapped and I told Joy that we were going to look for them. We made the stupid decision of going back to the house and breaking in. Next thing I knew, we were locked back down in the basement and both babies were there."

"Honey you don't have to say anymore."

"It's okay mom. Anyway he had his way with Joy and I again and that's how we became pregnant again. Later on another girl was thrown into the mix and her name was Sarah. At first she was like us but then he started feeding her with lies and she fed into them. He would tell her to do things and she would listen. They would stay upstairs and we would stay downstairs. One day she came in the room and I just had enough, so I hit her and I tied her up. I was able to get upstairs and I found a knife in the kitchen and I stabbed Chris and that's how we escaped. Hopefully he'll be put away for good this time."

Olivia's mom had tears in her eyes, "I'm so sorry sweetie."

"Mom don't worry, I think it's finally over now.

"We wanted to let you know that we did take Chris here to this hospital; he's in pretty bad shape but don't worry he's heavily guarded."

"What about the girl, Sarah?"

"We found her bound up and we also took her away. We really are very sorry about all this Ms. Mallor."

"Please just call me Olivia or Liv. What do you think is going to happen to Chris and Sarah?"

"They will stand trial for what they did. You and Joy might have to testify for what happened to the both of you."

"That's fine with me; I'd do anything to have them put away."

"We'll let you get your rest, if you need anything don't hesitate to call us."

172

"Thanks detectives, I really appreciate it." Olivia looked at her parents, "I really want to visit Joy now do you think you can take me mom?" Her mom helped her into the wheelchair and took her to see her. Joy was resting with her babies around her. Her mother was in the room, "Hi Ms. Monroe,"

"Hello Olivia." Joy looked happy to see her.

"How are you Joy?"

"I'm doing fine. They checked me and the babies out and everything is okay so I can go home tomorrow."

"They told me the same thing. Did you talk to the detectives?"

"Yeah they were here a little while ago."

"Okay I just spoke to them, we might have to testify."

"The detectives told me the same thing, I don't mind."

"Me neither."

"How are the babies Liv?"

"They are both doing great." Olivia walked towards Joy and hugged her tightly, "I'm so happy that we're all doing fine and that we never have to go back to that place ever again." They both cried in each other's arms.

*T*wenty-seven

A few months have gone by since Olivia and Joy escaped the hell that they were put through. Olivia and Joy decided that they would both get their GED's because they didn't want to go back to high school. Olivia was now nineteen and Joy was seventeen.

Olivia wanted to stay with her parents, she felt safer that way. Joy decided as well to stay with her mom but they kept in touch with each other. Olivia knew she wanted more in life so she decided to go to the local community college to be a nurse. Joy got a job with the bakery that was a few miles from home.

On the day of the trial, they both were really nervous.

"Liv I'm so scared, I really don't want to see Chris again."

"I know Joy but he'll never hurt us again. He's in custody and he'll be put away for a long time." Sarah had a different date, which they would have to testify for as well. When it was time for Olivia to go in, Joy wished her luck. She went in and she sat down in the box. The officer gave her the oath and she sat back down. The lawyer started asking her questions. A few times Olivia started crying but she made it through. When it was Joy's turn to testify the same thing happened, tears started to flow. After it was over they hugged each other. When it was time for the jurors to make their decision, Olivia and Joy were in the room waiting for the verdict. He was sentenced to fifty years in prison.

While the girls were held captive, Joe went to trial. From the evidence that they had collected, Joe was sentenced to fifteen years.

A few days later they had to be in court for Sarah's trial and once again they testified. Because she was a minor she was sentenced to juvenile hall for a minimum of five years. They were hoping for more but that was better than nothing.

"We can finally be in peace while those assholes rot in jail," said Joy.

"They should've gotten more but what's done is done. I hope they get raped in there just like they did to us." They looked at each other and smiled. They had their children and they felt free again.

One night Olivia was walking to her car from class and a man was standing there. She was afraid because she was alone and she didn't want what happened to her before, happen again.

"Can I help you?" She looked up and realized it was Detective Harrison. "Detective Harrison, you scared me! What are you doing here?"

"I'm sorry Ms. Mallor; I didn't mean to scare you."

"Is something wrong? Did Chris get out?"

"Oh no, he's in jail, I've actually been trying to reach you and you're a hard woman to track down," he smiled. This might sound a little funny but I was wondering if you wanted to get together some time?"

She smiled at him, "Do you mean like a date?"

"Yeah if you want to call it that," he smiled.

"Aren't you a little too old for me?"

"Actually I'm twenty-five; I was pretty new when I was assigned to your case."

"Okay I'll go out with you, if you call me by my name," she smiled.

"Of course Olivia, my name is Jake by the way."

"Hi Jake, it's nice to finally get your name."

"So, about that date, are you game for tomorrow night?"

"Okay, tomorrow night it is."

Jake walked over to her and kissed her hand, "It's a pleasure," and he walked away. Olivia was blushing. When Olivia got home, she felt like she was on cloud nine. She wondered if he was the one but she was a little nervous. Olivia walked into the house and there was a man waiting for her with her parents.

"Who is this?"

"Oh good Liv you're home. This is Mr. Daniel Cardigan he works for a publishing company.

He looked up at her and smiled, "It's nice to finally meet you Olivia. Your parents were telling me wonderful things about you."

"What can I help you with?"

"I was wondering if I can talk to you for a moment. I have something I would like to discuss with you."

"Sure, come in and sit down."

"Okay great. Well as you know, I'm with a publishing company and I was wondering if you wanted to write about what happened."

"You mean you want me to write a book about the ordeal Joy and I went through?"

"Yes exactly. Tell everyone your story, so another girl doesn't get attacked. You girls are heroes in a lot of women's eyes."

"I'll have to think about it."

"Sure no problem, take your time. If you feel more comfortable with Joy being around we can work that out, but I really want the story to come from you."

"Why me, Joy is just as good as I am?"

"I know for a fact that you're the stronger one Olivia, so I would really like to do this with you. Look I won't take up any more of your time, here is my card I would love to hear from you. It was nice to meet you Ms. Mallor." She got up and walked him out.

When he left, she looked at the card for a long time. She didn't know what to make of it, but this was the first time she was approached from someone about a book. Reporters always bugged her and Joy for stories but she didn't want to deal with them, but now that Chris was finally away, she thought maybe now is finally her chance.

Olivia sat down on the couch and her parents were looking at her, "What do you think about that?" Olivia asked.

"I think it might be a good opportunity to tell your story but it's up to you sweetheart."

"I don't know if Joy would like it if I did something like this or maybe she would get jealous."

"Why don't you call her and tell her about it?"

"Yeah that would be a good idea." Olivia checked on Lea and Elijah, they were sleeping. She walked into her room and decided now would be a good time to call Joy. The phone started ringing and Olivia was actually feeling kind of nervous. Joy picked up on the third ring.

"Hello."

"Hey Joy. It's Liv."

"Oh hey Liv, how are you?"

"I'm good. How are you?"

"I'm doing well, how has school been?"

"It's not too bad but I have something to talk to you about."

"Okay what's up?"

"A man was at my house tonight when I came home from class and he was waiting for me. He wants me to write a book about what happened."

"Wait so a guy comes out of nowhere and he asked you to write a book?"

Olivia smiled through the phone, "Yes and I kind of want to do it, but I wanted to run it by you first." Olivia felt excited for once.

"I don't know Liv, I'm not sure if it's a good idea."

"Why?"

"Because I am not sure if I'm ready for the public to hear what happened to us."

"Joy honesty I think everyone should hear what happened. It could save lives."

"Is that what he told you?"

"He didn't say it in those words Joy but I believe it would. A lot of women would want to hear about the encounters and how we lived to talk about it." Joy felt unsure; she wasn't ready for the world to hear what happened. She just wanted it all behind her. "I want to meet with him Joy and I want you to come with me. Pretty please Joy."

"Fine," said Joy.

The next day Olivia called Mr. Cardigan and set up a time to meet. She called her parents to see if they were available to take care of her children while her and Joy went out. When they pulled up to the café, Olivia spotted him right away. "Okay he's here let's do this," Olivia said. They got out of the car and walked inside. When they got to the table Daniel stood up.

"Hello Olivia it's nice to see you again and this must be Joy." He reached out his hand and Joy took it. "Please have a seat." They took a seat. "I'm very glad you called."

"We were unsure at first but I wanted to hear what you had to say."

"Of course, it's totally understandable. So what I was thinking is you would work with us and tell us everything that happened and we would pay you very generously for your time and for the book of course. I would give you a down payment now to start and then pay you when it's finished. What do you think?"

Olivia looked at Joy, "How much of a down payment?"

"How does ten thousand dollars sound?" They looked at each other and they couldn't believe it.

Joy turned to Olivia, "I don't know Liv. I think we should think about this."

"Are you crazy? That's a lot of money. We would have everything we need and we would be telling our story and every woman deserves to know what a sick bastard Chris, Joe, and Sarah were. We really should do this Joy." Joy just shook her head.

"What do you think Olivia?" asked Daniel.

"I'd say you have a deal." And she pulled her hand out to shake his hand.

"I would like for you to come to our offices tomorrow. Would that be okay?"

"Yes of course."

"Okay good I'll see you tomorrow, say ten?

"Sounds good, I'll see you tomorrow Daniel." He got up and left while Joy and Olivia remained seated.

"Are you sure you want to do this Liv?"

"Yes I'm sure. We need this; I think it would be good for us."

"I hope you know what you're doing."

"You should be happy that we're doing this."

"I am happy I just feel conflicted, maybe you're right. I just want to leave it all behind us."

"I know you do Joy." They decided to get a bite to eat and chat. "So I have something else I wanted to tell you Joy."

"Uh oh should I be afraid," she laughed.

"No," Olivia smiled. "Detective Harrison was at my college the other night; I guess he waited for me to be done. Anyway I was walking to my car and he was there and scared the living daylights out of me but then I realized it was him."

"Oh no, did something happen?" "That's exactly what I said when I saw him but no everything is fine. Anyway he asked me out." Olivia had a big smile on her face.

"Oh my God, are you serious? What did you say?"

"I told him yes so we're going out tonight. I'm pretty excited."

"Isn't he a little too old for you?"

Olivia laughed, "I said the same thing to him but it turns out he's twenty-five."

"Wow, that's so great Liv." Deep down Joy was a little disappointed. She had feelings for Olivia but couldn't say anything to her about it. When it was time for them to leave, they hugged each other and went their separate ways. Olivia drove home feeling exhilarated, she finally felt alive and excited for once in her life. When she got home, she told her parents all about it. They screamed for joy and decided to celebrate. They were so happy for her.

*T*wenty-eight

*O*livia was nervous for her date tonight with Jake but she was ready for it. She heard someone knocking at the front door. Her mom answered the door to greet him.

"Hello Detective Harrison, it's good to see you again."

"Please Mrs. Mallor, call me Jake."

"Okay Jake," she smiled. "I'll be right back I'll get Olivia for you, please have a seat."

"Thank you."

Olivia's mom knocked on her bedroom door, "He's here honey."

"Okay I'll be right there." Olivia came out and Jake stood up; he was holding a dozen roses.

"Thank you so much Jake! You didn't have to do this."

187

"You deserve it," and he smiled. She took the roses and handed them to her mom so she could put them in water.

"I'll see you later mom."

"Okay be careful you two." They walked out to the car and Jake opened the door for her. Olivia got in and buckled up.

Jake got in, buckled up and looked at her, "You look beautiful."

Olivia blushed and smiled, "Thank you." Jake pulled out of the driveway and they drove to a quaint little restaurant on the edge of town. He pulled up and got out and opened the door for her.

"I hope you're hungry," he said.

"Actually I am starved." They walked in and it was popping. The music was lively and she immediately felt relaxed. The host sat them right away. "How do you know about this place?" She asked.

"Being a cop I kind of know the ropes." She laughed. "You know I was afraid to ask you out, I

188

wanted to wait a few months after everything blew over."

"It's totally fine I'm glad you did. So tell me how did you become a detective?"

"Well it just sort of happened. My family comes from a long line of cops, so it was inevitable that I was going to be one."

"That makes sense." The waiter showed up and they ordered their drinks and food.

"So Olivia, tell me about you. Like what do you like to do for fun?"

"Oh you mean besides taking care of my children?" she smiled. "Hmm let me think, I like to read, watch movies, draw, dance, you know whatever I guess. What about you?"

"Hmm I like movies, art, traveling, and basically what you said. How are your children by the way?"

"They're doing very well, thank you for asking. I'm surprised you would want to get involved with someone that has children."

"Having a child wouldn't push me away. I knew when I met you that there was something special about you. I know you were young and it wasn't like it just hit me. The more time I spent with you and getting to know you, the more my feelings for you blossomed." Olivia felt giddy inside, but she was kind of stand offish. The last time she gave her heart to someone; he kidnapped and raped her.

"I'm really happy you told me all that. I get kind of worried and nervous because of Chris."

"I totally understand Olivia and we can take it really slow. I don't mind. I just want to get to know you." Olivia smiled.

When dinner was over, Jake asked Olivia, "Do you mind if I take you somewhere? There's a place I want to show you." She was hesitant at first but then she accepted. Jake drove her to a nearby lake. It was dark and the moon was so bright it reflected off of the water.

"This is breathtaking Jake."

"I thought you might like it here. Have you ever been here before?"

"No but it looks vaguely familiar." She looked down a ways and saw the covered bridge, the one where she was going to throw herself off of. Her face turned solemn.

"What's the matter?"

"I just realized that I have been here before; down a little ways is the bridge where I met Chris. You know he saved my life."

"How did he save your life?" She wasn't sure she wanted to share this with him but she felt like she could tell him anything.

"A while back I was thinking about committing suicide, I was stupid and naive. Anyway, I woke up one morning before school and decided to go to that bridge and throw myself off of it. I was about to jump when Chris appeared, he actually pulled me back and the rest is history."

"I'm glad he saved your life but I'm not happy for what he did to you and I'm very sorry for that."

"It's okay; we wouldn't have met if that didn't happen. I mean I prefer that didn't happen at all but very happy to have met you."

"I really do like you Olivia."

"You can call me Liv and I really do like you too." She felt him staring at her. There was a slight breeze blowing and he pulled the hair away from her eyes.

"You really are beautiful." She smiled at him and he turned her in his direction and kissed her. When she stopped kissing him, she felt at that moment that this could be the man of her dreams. Jake was smiling at her and he took her hand and kissed it. "You really are something Olivia Mallor. Come on let's go time to get you home." He grabbed her hand and they walked back to the car. He opened the door for her and she got in. Jake got in beside her and they left to go back to her house. Out front he parked the car, "I'll walk you to the door." He got out and opened the door for her and he walked her to the front door.

"I had a really good time with you Jake, thank you so much for everything."

"It was my pleasure; I hope we can do it again soon."

"I think that can be arranged" she smiled.

"Can I kiss you goodnight?" She shook her head yes. He leaned in and kissed her for a second time and this time she saw fireworks. They pulled away from each other and said goodnight. Olivia watched him get back in the car and leave; she walked into the house feeling something she never felt before.

Her mom was in the living room, "Hey how did the date go?"

Olivia couldn't help but smile, "It was amazing. I think he might be the one."

Her mom smiled at her, "For your sake Liv I hope you're right. He seems like a keeper."

"He definitely seems to be." Olivia checked on her babies and saw that Lea was awake and she was starting to talk. "Hey baby." She picked her up and held her tightly. She gave her a kiss and put her down. "You should be sleeping Lea, let's get you back in bed." She tucked her in and kissed her goodnight then she walked over to baby Elijah and saw he was sleeping; she leaned down and kissed him. She went to her room and went to sleep. It will be the most peaceful sleep she will have in a long time.

*T*wenty-nine

Olivia felt like the last few weeks were flying by. She had been in contact with the publishing company about the book she and Joy were working on. Her relationship with Jake was soaring, which she was happy about. Her children were doing very well, Lea was walking up a storm and she was talking a lot. Elijah was starting to walk now as well so now she had to keep a watchful eye on them both. Her parents were wonderful for helping with them and Jake loved being around them. Olivia wanted to spend some time with Joy. They hadn't really been spending time together with the exception of the book they were writing so she decided to call her to see if she wanted to get together. The phone rang and Joy finally answered it.

"Hey Joy, I was wondering if you wanted to get together for lunch or something?" Joy seemed hesitant at first but decided that it was okay.

"Sure Liv, where do you want to meet up?"

"How about at Havana, you know where that is right?"

"Yeah, I'll be there."

"Okay good, I'll see you around twelve thirty?"

"Okay sounds good, see you then." Olivia hung up and she felt like something was wrong with Joy but then dismissed it. She went in to her kid's bedroom to change them and dress them. She brought them into the kitchen for breakfast.

"Good morning mom and dad."

"Good morning Liv, how are you this morning?"

"I'm good, how are you guys?"

"We're doing fine; your father is about to head to work though."

"That's a shame dad but I hope you have a good day."

"Thanks you too honey." Her dad left the house and Olivia sat down at the table to feed the kid's.

"Hey mom can I ask you something?"

"Of course ask away."

"I think there is something wrong with Joy. Ever since I started dating Jake she seems like depressed. Do you think she's mad at me or something?"

"I don't see why she would be, she should be happy for you."

"I guess you're right, she just seems off. I'm meeting her for lunch today at Havana. Would you mind watching the kid's for me?"

"Of course not, I love having them all to myself."

"Thanks mom." Olivia finished feeding the kids and placed them in their playpens. She went and got a shower and got dressed. Her phone started to ring, it was Jake.

"Hey beautiful, I just wanted to check in with you and see how you're doing."

"Aw aren't you the sweetest. I'm doing great; I'm actually getting ready to meet Joy for lunch at Havana. Are you doing alright?"

"Now that I'm talking to you I'm doing very well, thanks for asking."

"How's work going?"

"It's alright, you know how it is."

Olivia laughed, "Well I got to run Jake, am I seeing you later?"

"Of course you are beautiful unless you don't want to."

"Of course I want to silly."

"Have a good lunch and tell Joy I said hello."

"I will," and Olivia hung up.

When Olivia pulled up to the restaurant she saw Joy standing waiting for her. She got out of the car and met up with her. They said their hellos and hugged each other. They were shown a spot in the back and sat down.

"Is something wrong Olivia?"

"Of course not, I just missed you. I feel like we don't see each other that often anymore except for writing the book."

"Oh okay."

"Are you alright Joy? You don't seem like yourself these days."

"Actually Liv, I have to tell you something and you're not going to like it." Olivia made a face; she knew this couldn't be good. "I've decided I'm moving away from here."

"What do you mean?"

"I'm sorry but I need to get away from here. My dad lives in Oklahoma so I decided to go and live with him."

"But I thought we were going to write this book together and we even made a pact to always be together here in Asheville."

"I know but I really can't take it here anymore. I feel like I'm always reminded of Chris and I don't want that. I just want to be far away from here."

"Are you sure it's not because of me dating Jake?" Joy looked at her and looked away. "Okay what was that look for Joy? Do you have feelings for Jake, is that it? Are you mad at me for dating him?"

Joy looked up with tears in her eyes, "Actually Liv, I have feelings for you. I'm in love with you." Olivia looked shocked; she couldn't believe what she was hearing.

"What do you mean you're in love with me Joy?"

"I've been in love with you for a long time, ever since we were together at the house. You're the first and only person I trusted when it came to anyone after the whole incident. I'm sorry Liv, it doesn't matter anymore. I have to go."

"You really can't talk to me about this Joy?"

"The only reason I agreed to see you is because I wanted to tell you that I'm leaving. I'm sorry but I can't be here anymore, finish the book without me," Joy got up and left. Olivia had tears in her eyes; her best friend had just left her. One minute she was on top of the world, the next she felt like she sunk right to the bottom. She needed to talk to Jake; he was her person when she was upset.

She dialed his number and he picked up, "Harrison."

"Jake it's me."

"Olivia are you alright, you sound upset."

"It's Joy, she's leaving she said she's moving to Oklahoma."

"Why, did she give you a reason?"

"She said it was because of me, she told me she is in love with me."

"Really, wow!"

"Yeah, I'm so upset."

"Do you need me to leave work? I can be there in ten minutes."

"No Jake it's alright I should go home. My mom is there with the kids so I should be there. I'll see you later, thanks for listening."

"Okay babe, I'll see you soon." Olivia hung up the phone and went home. When she walked in she saw her mom playing with the kids.

"I'm home mom, thanks for watching them for me."

"No problem sweetie, hey are you alright?"

"Yeah mom I'm fine. I just found out that Joy is leaving to go live with her father in Oklahoma. I didn't even know that she had a father that lived there."

"Did she say why she was leaving?" Olivia didn't want to tell her the truth about why she was leaving. "She told me she couldn't handle living around here anymore because of Chris. She said it was too many memories."

"I'm so sorry honey. I know she was your best friend and you went through so much together." She walked over to Olivia and hugged her.

Thirty

A few months had passed since Joy left and Olivia was still trying to get over it. She rarely heard from her. Olivia would make an effort to contact her. She tried to call her, mail her, and even email but she couldn't get a hold of her.

Olivia and Jake were spending a lot of time together since Joy was no longer around. Olivia was keeping up with the writing of her book so that would help keep her busy. Olivia was finishing up for the night when the phone rang and it was Jake.

"Hey beautiful, can you come outside?"

"You're outside?"

"Yes can you come out and see me?"

"Of course, I'll be right out." Olivia hung up the phone, closed down her laptop and went outside to see Jake. He looked amazing, something about him was different but she wasn't sure what. She went up to him and kissed him, "Hey, what's up with the surprise visit?"

"I just wanted to see you; I actually wanted to talk to you about something." Olivia's face fell; she thought he was breaking up with her. "Please tell me you're not breaking up with me."

"Of course not, actually the opposite. Here sit down." She took a seat on the porch. "I was wondering if we could take our relationship to the next level."

"What do you mean?"

"I was wondering if you and your children would move in with me." She looked at him and couldn't believe what she was hearing, her smile lit up her face.

"Are you serious?"

"Yes, I've been thinking about it for awhile and I really want you with me. I want to go to sleep every night with you and wake up every morning to your beautiful face."

"I can't believe this; I really don't know what to say."

"Say yes silly."

"Of course we'll move in with you!" She hugged him and kissed him slowly. "Oh my God I'm so excited."

"I love you Olivia."

"I love you Jake." Olivia got up and took Jake's hand and pulled him in the house. The kids were sleeping and her parents were out at a fundraiser so they had the house to themselves. Olivia pulled him to her bedroom and closed the door. She started to kiss him and he stopped her.

"We don't have to Liv; I don't want to rush anything."

"I want to Jake." She kissed him again, first it was slowly and then it became more passionate. When he realized that she wanted him, he too became more passionate. She took off his shirt and felt his chest; he lifted her arms and slowly slipped her top off.

They both lay down on the bed, "Are you sure you want to do this?"

"Yes I'm sure."

He removed her pants and looked at her, "You're so beautiful." She leaned up and kissed his mouth and went down to his chest, he unbuckled his pants and pulled his pants off. Jake peeled off her panties and slipped her bra off. Jake laid her down and kissed her. He started kissing her chest and slowly made his way down, she was moaning in ecstasy. She never knew what this was really like. She was always forced into sex and she was nervous but excited at the same time. She reached up for him and pulled him towards her. She kissed his lips and they tasted salty from her. He slipped inside her easily and slowly.

"You okay baby?"

"Yes," she whispered. It felt so right to Olivia that tears were forming in her eyes; she never felt something so amazing to her.

After they made love, Jake leaned over her and kissed her, "I love you so much Liv."

She kissed him back, "I love you Jake." They fell asleep holding each other. Olivia woke up and saw that Jake was still there and she smiled. She got up quietly and went to the bathroom. She decided to check on her babies. She saw that Elijah was stirring so she went to him, picked him up, and fed him with her breast. She felt an arm go around her and she squealed, when she turned around it was Jake. "Are you okay? It's only me baby."

"I'm sorry. You scared me, the nights are still hard on me and I always think Chris is going to come out of nowhere."

"You don't have to worry about that anymore Liv. I'm here for you now and we'll be living together so I'll always be here. I'll keep you safe. He's in prison Liv."

"I know he is, thank God. I'm so grateful I have you in my life." He smiled and kissed her tenderly.

"Come on, come back to bed." She was done feeding Elijah and put him back down and she walked back to the bedroom. They climbed back into bed and lay down and she fell asleep with his arm around her.

The next morning she woke up and saw Jake staring at her.

"What are you looking at?" she laughed.

"I can't wait to wake up to you every morning," he smiled.

"Come on I'll make you breakfast, plus you probably want to tell your parents the good news." They got up and went to the kitchen. Olivia's mom and dad were both in the kitchen when they walked in.

"Good morning Liv and good morning Jake. I didn't know you were staying over last night."

"Sorry mom it just sort of happened. We have some news to tell you."

"What kind of news?"

"Jake asked me to move in with him and I gladly accepted."

"Oh honey I'm so happy for you." She hugged her and her dad got up and hugged her. Then they both hugged Jake.

"Thank you Mr. and Mrs. Mallor for letting me have her."

"Oh Jake you're wonderful to our daughter. I just hope one day you make an honest woman out of her."

Jake laughed, "One day sir."

"I know you will Jake."

Jake turned to Olivia and kissed her, "I have to run cutie. I have to get to work but I'll talk to you later about the arrangements."

"Okay Jake, I love you."

"I love you too sugar." Jake left the house and Olivia turned her attention to her parents, who were so happy for her.

"When do you plan on leaving?"

"I don't know we didn't discuss details yet, we will later. He just asked me last night."

"We're happy for you Liv, you and the kids deserve happiness."

"Thank you so much guys." Olivia went to her kid's room and saw Lea standing on the bed, "Guess what Lea, we're moving in with Jake." Lea looked at her and smiled. She got Lea up and picked up Elijah, she fed them and changed them. Olivia had to get ready to go to class; she got a shower and got dressed.

"Alright mom, I have to go to class, you don't mind watching Lea and Elijah do you?"

"Of course not, I'll see you after class."

Thirty-one

When Olivia was finished with class she wanted to call Joy and tell her the good news. She sat in the cafeteria and dialed Joy's number.

"Hello."

"Joy is that you?"

"Olivia?"

"Hey Joy, how are you? You don't sound too good. I've been trying to reach you."

"I know Liv, I'm sorry I just haven't been able to get to the phone."

"Is everything alright?"

"Well it turns out I've been sick Liv?"

"What do you mean?"

"I have cancer Liv." Olivia was stunned; she was speechless. "Are you there Liv?"

"Yeah I'm here, what kind of cancer? Is it bad?"

"I have colon cancer, it's pretty bad and my daddy has been doing everything in his power to help me."

"I'm so sorry Joy. How are your little ones holding up?"

"My dad has been taking care of them."

"Oh Joy I feel so awful. Is there anything I can do?"

"There's nothing you can do Liv, thanks for asking though. So what's new with you?"

"Well I wanted to tell you that Jake and I have decided to move in together." Joy started coughing. "Are you alright Joy?"

"Sorry about that, yeah I'm okay, that's great Liv."

"Thanks Joy."

"I have to go Liv I'm sorry; I'll talk to you soon."

"Oh okay Joy." All Olivia heard was a click. She felt awful; she didn't know what she could do

212

though to help her. Her best friend was dying and she was devastated, she felt like she had to go and see her.

When she got home from class she told her mom the news of Joy.

"Mom I want to go and see her."

"Do you think that's a good idea? Did she say she wanted you to visit?"

"Well no, but maybe if I surprise her, maybe it will make her feel better."

"I don't know Liv that's a big deal and the way you said she sounded, it sounds like she doesn't want to see you. I know that's hard for you to understand but she has her reasons."

"I know mom but I really want to see her. If she's dying, I would like to at least say goodbye. I thought she would at least want to see me." Olivia started to cry, her mom held her tightly.

"I know baby." Later that night someone knocked on the door and it was Jake.

Olivia opened the door and hugged him immediately, "Hello there gorgeous," and he hugged her back. When she let go he could tell something was wrong. "What's the matter babe?"

"I called Joy today to let her know about my news."

"Yeah and how did she take it?"

"She said she was happy for me but it sure didn't sound like it. She also sounded awful, it turns out that she's sick. She has colon cancer."

"Oh babe I'm so sorry." He took her in his arms and held her tightly while she cried on his shoulder.

"I wanted to go and see her but my mom thinks that might be a bad idea. What do you think?"

"You said she didn't sound like she wanted to see you or even talk to you."

"I know but she's my best friend, I feel like I have a right to see her."

"I know Liv but you have to give her space. If she doesn't want to see you then maybe you shouldn't."

"I guess you're right."

"So let's talk about something positive. Let's talk about you moving in with me." She smiled.

"Okay. When are you thinking you want to do this?" she asked."

Jake looked at her, "I'm thinking this weekend we can start moving your stuff over."

Olivia laughed and hugged him tightly, "You got it."

"Okay great! Do you want to get something to eat?"

"I'm thinking I want to stay home, I don't really feel up to going out, I'm sorry."

"It's okay, I understand. So where are the little ones?"

She got up and went out of the room, "They're in here." He walked in the playroom and greeted Lea and Elijah.

Lea was happy to see him; she walked up to him and hugged him, "Did mommy tell you that y'all are going to live with me?"

Lea smiled, and said, "Yeah."

"Good, are you excited?"

She yelled, "Excited." They all laughed.

Olivia wanted to put them to bed so she got them all ready and tucked them in. Jake helped and they both kissed them goodnight. They left the room and quietly went into her bedroom.

"Do you want to stay over tonight?"

He smiled, "I don't think that would be a good idea, your dad didn't seem too happy that I was here last night. We'll be together this weekend finally and then we can go to bed and wake up together.

She kissed him gently, "You're too good for me and I don't know what I did to deserve you."

"It's just you being you Liv, now I better go and let you sleep. I'll see you tomorrow."

She looked disappointed but she understood, "Okay Jake, I love you."

"I love you too." When he left she settled down for the night and went to sleep.

That night she had a horrible dream about Chris. He took her again and raped her multiple times and then killed her. She woke herself up crying. "I wonder if this will ever stop," she said to herself. She got up out of bed and it was still dark outside. She made her way to the kid's room and checked on them and they were sleeping peacefully. She walked into the kitchen and got a glass of water. She looked through the window and she swore she saw someone staring at her. She dropped the glass of water and it shattered all over the floor. Her mother turned the light on and came running to her.

"What's the matter, what happened?"

"I thought I saw someone watching me out the window, I got scared."

Her mom went to look out the window, "I don't see anyone sweetie, maybe you thought you did."

"I swear I saw someone."

"I didn't see anyone, here sit down, I'll make you some tea."

Olivia sat down, "Mom I don't know how much longer I can do this. I keep having nightmares and I can't sleep at night. Maybe Joy was right to move away."

"You may think that Liv but you can't run away from your problems, you should face them. Maybe it's time you see someone, like a therapist, it may help. I think with you writing the book, it's causing you to flashback to all the things that you've been through. It's only a suggestion."

"I'll think about it." The tea was whistling and her mom ran over to prepare the tea for Olivia.

"Here you go honey."

"Thanks." They sat there in silence for a while. "Do you think it's a good idea to move in with Jake?"

Her mom looked up at her and smiled, "I think Jake is a very good man and he's very good to you and those kids. I think you're lucky you have him around. So yes, I think it's a good idea." Olivia smiled, that made her feel better.

"I think it's a good idea too. We decided that this weekend I'll move in. Can you help me?"

"Of course honey."

When Olivia was done with her tea she put her cup in the sink and kissed her mom, "I think I'll try and go back to bed. Thanks for the tea."

"You're welcome Liv; I'll see you in the morning." They walked out of the kitchen and went back to their bedrooms. Olivia lay down and she finally had good dreams about her babies and of Jake.

Thirty-two

The next morning Olivia woke up and she felt more rested. She took care of her babies and had to get to class. When she got to class she felt good, like things were beginning to get better. She had her babies, had an amazing boyfriend and she was moving in with him. She was still upset about Joy but there was nothing she could do about it, she still couldn't believe she was dying. In that moment she thought to herself, "I need to see her; I can't just let it go." She decided that she was going so she called Jake when class was over.

"Jake, I need to see Joy; I'm going to fly out to see her."

"If you really need to then you should go but I'm coming with you. I can't let you go alone, not after everything that has happened."

"You really don't have to Jake."

"I know I don't have to Liv but I want to."

She smiled, "Okay, I'm leaving here and I'm going home to ask my parents to watch the kids, and then I'm getting tickets."

"Okay babe, I'll let work know I have some business to take care of, I'll see you at your house."

"Okay babe." She hung up the phone and drove home. When she got to her house Jake was waiting for her. They walked into the house to see her parents.

"Mom, I'm home."

Her mom called out to her, "We're in the playroom."

They walked into the playroom and greeted the kids, "Are you having fun with Gigi?" They both smiled and laughed; they were running all over the room. "Mom I was wondering if you could do me a favor."

"Uh oh what is it?"

"I was wondering if you could take care of the kids for a day or two. I need to see Joy; Jake is coming with me to make sure everything goes okay."

"So you're really going to go? If you really feel like you need to then yes I'll watch them for you."

"I really need to do this mom, thank you so much!" She hugged her and kissed her.

"When are you leaving?"

"I'm going to look at flights now to see when the first one to Oklahoma is."

"Okay." They walked to her room and shut the door; she turned on the laptop and checked for flights, the next one going out was tomorrow morning, so she booked it.

"I guess I'll stay with you tonight, since we have to leave early in the morning. Are you going to call Joy and tell her?"

"I think I'm going to call her when I actually get to her town. So that way she can't turn me away. I have to tell my parents, I'll be right back." Olivia walked into the playroom and told her mom that they were leaving early in the morning, "Do you mind if Jake stays over?"

"Sure he can stay over."

"Thanks mom, I appreciate all you do for me." She smiled at her. Olivia went back to her bedroom; "I want to spend some time with the kids before I go." They both walked back to the playroom and played with the kids. When it was time for bed, they both got them ready. She told Lea that she was leaving for a couple days and that Gigi and Grandpa were going to take care of her and Elijah. They both kissed them goodnight and closed the door.

They went back to her bedroom and lay down, "Thanks for being here for me Jake."

"Of course, there isn't anywhere else I would rather be."

She leaned over and kissed him, "I want you." She slid off her clothes and climbed on top of him. He ran his fingers through her hair. He took off his boxers and she slid herself onto him, she let out a quiet moan. She started to move quickly, he grabbed her and turned her on her back.

"You're killing me Liv." She smiled up at him, he quickly put himself into her and she moaned in ecstasy. "You like that baby?"

"Uh huh," she answered breathlessly. After they finished, they lay there holding each other until they fell asleep.

In the morning, they woke up, got dressed and kissed her babies goodbye. They left the house and headed for the airport. The plane was scheduled to leave at 5:05 a.m. When they got to the airport they decided to get something for breakfast and waited for their flight to be called. At four thirty, their flight was called and they boarded. The flight was going to Tulsa and it would take a few hours to get there.

"This is my first time flying, I'm really nervous," said Olivia.

"We'll be fine Liv; I'll hold your hand the whole time." She laughed. When it was time for the plane to go down the runway, she squeezed Jake's hand. The plane took off, "Don't break my hand," Jake laughed.

"Oh I'm sorry," she smiled. When the plane was settled and flying toward their destination, she realized it wasn't as bad as she thought. A few hours later the plane landed. They got off and found a taxi to take them to the nearest hotel. When they arrived, they were exhausted but Olivia knew she had to see Joy. Jake went in to take a shower and she dialed her number. On the third ring, Joy answered.

"Hey Joy."

"Oh hi Olivia, what's up?"

"I need to see you."

"That's kind of hard don't you think since I'm here and you're in North Carolina."

"Well I wanted to tell you but I wanted it to be a surprise kind of, I'm here in Tulsa."

"You're where?"

"I'm here in Tulsa; I thought I would surprise you."

"Jeez Liv, you can't just show up here." "I'm sorry but if I called you when I was home to tell you I'm coming over you would've said no."

225

"Well I'm still saying no," and she hung up. Olivia was sitting on the bed when Jake came out.

"Is everything okay, did you call her?"

"Yeah I did and she doesn't want to see me."

"I knew this was a bad idea. I guess we should head back home." "No way, I'm going to see her anyway."

"Do you know her address?"

"No, but I'll find out."

"And how do you expect to do that?" She smiled up at him, "Uh oh what are you thinking?"

"I'm thinking you're a detective so why don't you put your skills to work," she laughed.

"Oh so you want to use me," he smiled. She pulled him down on the bed and pulled off the towel he was wearing. She kissed his lips and then kissed his chest and then she slowly went further down. He started moaning and shaking. "You're a bad girl."

"Yeah but you love me."

"I sure as hell do. I'll see what I can do. What is her father's name again?"

"His name is Charles, Charles Monroe." Jake made a few phone calls and as it turned out it was easier than he thought to get the address. In the morning they would go and see her.

Thirty-three

*I*n the morning Olivia was the first to rise. She got up, went to the bathroom and showered. When she got out Jake was up and making coffee.

"Good morning gorgeous."

"Good morning." She walked over to him and kissed him. "Thanks for making coffee," she smiled.

"You're welcome babe." He found a cup and went over to the sink and rinsed it out. He poured the coffee for her, added some sugar, and some powdered creamer.

"Wow that looks yummy," she laughed.

"It was all they had in these stupid little packets."

"It's alright; I'm only messing with you."

"So have you figured out how you want to go about seeing Joy today?"

"I thought we would get some breakfast and then go out to see her. I would like to see her ASAP."

"Alright I can roll with that; I saw a café not too far from here."

"You wanted to walk there?"

"Sure why not it's right up the road."

"Okay Mr. Adventuress, I'll take a walk with you. Just let me take this crappy cup of coffee and pour it down the drain," she smiled.

They both got dressed and headed down the road to the café.

Just then a pickup truck pulled up, "Hey can I give you a lift?"

"Sure that would be great."

"Where are you heading?"

"We're going to the café down the street."

"Oh okay, that's Peggy's place. Are you from out of town?"

"Yeah we're from North Carolina."

"What are you doing around these parts if you don't mind me asking?"

"I'm here to visit a friend and Jake here is just tagging along."

"I gotcha, my name is Rick."

"I'm Olivia and this is Jake."

"Nice to meet you folks and here we are."

"Thanks for the ride Rick and it was nice to meet you."

"It was nice to meet you folks." They got out of the truck and went into the café. When they walked in, the heat smacked them right in the face. A woman with a grey beehive was at the counter, her nametag read June.

"Can I help you two?"

"We're here to get something to eat."

"Okay you can sit anywhere you want," and she walked away. When they found a spot, they sat down and looked over the menus. The same woman that told them to sit anywhere reappeared and asked what they wanted.

"We'll just have two coffees and two bagels with cream cheese," Jake said. The woman walked away without saying anything.

"She seems like a nice woman," Olivia smiled. When their food arrived they ate it quickly and hailed a cab to Tulsa.

When they arrived on the street of Joy's address, Olivia felt a little nervous but she needed to see her. The taxi pulled up out front of Joy's house. They paid the guy and got out of the car. They walked up to the house holding hands.

"I'm really nervous Jake, what if she slams the door in my face?"

"Then we'll leave."

She took a deep breath and exhaled, "Here we go." She knocked on the door and a man answered.

"Yes can I help you?"

"Hi are you Mr. Monroe?"

"What's it to you?"

"I'm Olivia and this is Jake and we were wondering if Joy is here?"

"Oh Olivia, it's nice to finally meet you I heard a lot about you. Welcome to my home, please come in." When they walked in they couldn't believe their eyes. The house was beautiful; it had marble floors and a chandelier hung from the ceiling. The walls were decorated with exquisite art.

"Wow Mr. Monroe, your house is beautiful."

"Thanks, it's the wife that decorated it."

"Well she did an amazing job."

He smiled at her, "Oh you're here for Joy; she's out back. It's Just down the hallway there and its straight back."

"Okay thank you." They walked down the hallway and out the back door and they saw someone swimming in the in ground pool. "That can't be Joy; she's supposed to be real sick." When they walked closer they realized that it was Joy. They walked over to the pool and Joy looked up and realized they were standing there. "Hello Joy," Olivia said.

"Olivia what are you doing here? I told you not to come."

"I wanted to come and see you, you sounded awful on the phone. I thought you didn't have much time left and here you are swimming in the pool. What gives Joy?" Olivia sounded hurt. Joy got up out of the pool and grabbed a towel and wrapped it around herself.

"Come let's sit down. Do either of you want a drink?" Both of them shook their heads. "Fine have it your way." She grabbed a drink from the mini fridge on the deck and sat down.

Joy was just staring into space, "Well, are you going to say anything or what?"

"Liv, I lied to you."

"Why would you lie to me?"

"I didn't want to see or speak to you anymore. I just wanted to live my life Liv."

"Okay, well if you didn't want to see me or speak to me you could've just said that. I was worried about you and I wanted to come and express my sympathy to you. We went through a lot together and you were my best friend. I can't believe you lied to me."

"I'm sorry Liv it was the only way I felt like I could get away from you." Olivia looked like she was on the verge of tears, Jake grabbed her hand and she looked at him and smiled.

"I see. Well I guess it's time for me to leave, I overstayed my welcome." Olivia got up and started to walk to the door that led into the house.

"Olivia, wait a minute!" Joy got up and grabbed her arm. "Please don't leave, sit down." Olivia looked at Jake and he didn't say anything but she knew that look, so she sat down.

Jake knelt down besides her, "I'm going to wait out front for you. I think it would be good for you two to talk alone." He kissed her forehead and walked back in the house.

Joy smiled at Olivia, "I can't believe you two are together. It's crazy how things work out."

"Yeah I know I'm really happy."

"I'm happy for you Liv," Joy said. Joy leaned over towards her, "Don't worry about what I told you before Liv. I'm sorry I even said that to you. You're my best friend and I don't ever want to lose that."

Olivia was fiddling with her fingers and then looked up at her, "How could I forget about what you said? I will never forget it." "Let's just drop it." They both looked away from each other. The friendship between them was fading.

"Where are the kids? I haven't seen them around here."

Joy looked up at her with a sad face, "I actually left them with my mom."

Olivia looked shocked, "But they're your children, I thought you couldn't part from them."

Joy gave her a look and cried out, "I couldn't take care of them Liv, they are better off without me."

"How could you say that? There is nothing like a bond between a child and a parent. They need you! I could never leave my children behind."

"I'm not you Liv."

Olivia got up, "You're right you're not me," and she got up and walked back in the house and out the front door.

Thirty-four

When Olivia walked out the front door she saw Jake leaning against a taxi.

She ran to him and put her arms around him, "I love you Jake," and she kissed him.

When she released him he looked at her, "What was that for?"

"I'm just happy to have you in my life and I can't wait to move in with you. Now let's get out of here." She got in the taxi and Jake got in next to her.

"You okay, did everything go alright in there?"

Olivia started to have tears in her eyes. "I'm done Jake. I just want to go home to my children."

She didn't have to say anymore, he looked at the driver, "You can go now," and they went down the street and back to the hotel.

When they arrived back at the hotel, they asked the taxi to wait; they wanted to get to the airport. They gathered their stuff and loaded it in the trunk and went to the airport.

When they arrived at the airport, Jake paid the guy and they grabbed their stuff and headed inside.

They sat down to wait for their flight, "So do you want to talk to me about it Liv?"

She looked at him, "I know that Chris really messed her head up but he messed up mine too. I just don't know how she could leave her children behind."

"What do you mean?"

"She left her kids with her mom and she came here. She said she couldn't take care of them. I could never leave my children, ever."

Jake took her hand, "I'm sure she had her reasons Liv. She didn't seem like she was taking it very well but I do understand where you're coming from." Just then the announcement came on for the passengers to board. They got up and walked to the gate to get on the plane. They sat down on the plane and she just stared out the window. "Are you going to be okay baby?"

She turned her head to him, "Yeah I'll be fine," and she smiled. When they landed, they got back into his car and headed back to her house. When they arrived it was evening, "Do you want to come in?"

"I think I better let you go in there alone. I'm tired and I think you should spend some one on one time with your kids. I'll see you tomorrow gorgeous."

She looked at him and smiled, "Goodnight Jake."

"Tomorrow is the big day and then we'll be together every day," he smiled. She kissed him good night and got out of the car.

She walked into the house, "I'm home." Her kids came running to her and hugged her tightly. "I missed you both very much."

"We missed you mommy," Lea said. "Where are Gigi and Grandpa?" Lea pointed towards the kitchen. She picked up Elijah and walked in the kitchen with Lea on her trail. She saw her parents sitting at the kitchen table smiling at each other, and then they looked up.

"Hey honey," her mom said. "How did it go?" Olivia plopped herself down on the chair next to her dad and put Elijah on her lap. Lea walked over to sit on her Gigi's lap.

"Well we saw her and she lied to me. She wasn't sick at all. She just didn't want to see me or speak to me anymore." Olivia started to get tears in her eyes but she wasn't ready to let them fall.

"Oh honey I'm sorry to hear that, I can't believe she would lie to you like that. You must be really upset."

"You know what, I thought I was going to be but I'm really not. She's the one that decided to cut me out of her life and she also decided to cut her kids out of her life. She left them with her mom here in town."

Her mom looked stunned, "Her children are with her mother?"

Olivia looked over at her, "Yeah can you imagine?" and she looked at her children. "I could never leave my babies behind." They spoke a little more and then Olivia got up to get the kids ready for bed. While giving the kids a bath, she told them that she loved them very much and would never leave them. She dressed them in their PJ's and put them to bed. She walked out into the living room and sat down with her parents.

"Tomorrow is the big day," Olivia said.

Her mom smiled, "I'm going to miss you around here and those kids of yours of course."

"Mom, you can see them anytime you want to and I would hope you would babysit for us sometimes."

"Of course honey, I would love too, I love those babies."

She gave her mom a hug, "I better get to bed I think Jake wants to get started early on the moving process."

"I think that's because he's excited to have you all to himself." Olivia laughed and got up and went into the bathroom. She looked at herself for a long time and she realized for the first time that she was truly happy even if Joy wasn't going to be a part of it anymore.

Olivia was sleeping when she felt as if someone was staring at her and she jolted awake.

"Whoa there Liv, it's only me."

"Jeez you scared the hell out of me Jake."

He leaned over her and kissed her forehead, "I'm sorry baby. Here I brought you a coffee."

"Thanks babe but you know how I get so please try not to scare me like that."

"I know I shouldn't have done that. I just enjoy watching you sleep."

She smiled at him and took a sip of her coffee, "This is delicious, thanks Jake."

"Are you ready for the big move?"

"More than ever," she beamed at him. "Have to get up and get ready." She got up and went to the bathroom and brushed her teeth. She went back in her bedroom and Jake was kneeling down, "Oh my God, Jake." He presented a ring to her. She clasped her hand to her mouth, "Jake what are you doing?"

"Olivia Mallor, I know we haven't been together long but I love you. I love you more than anything in this world and I want to take care of you and your children. Make me the happiest man alive and marry me."

Olivia couldn't believe it, tears were streaming down her cheeks, "Of course Jake," she took him in her arms and squeezed him. "You're the best thing to ever happen to me, I mean besides my kids," she laughed. "Was this your plan?" she smiled.

"I really wanted to ask you, so I figured now is the perfect time then any," he smiled back.

"I have to tell my parents," she screamed in happiness. "Mom, dad, look what just happened!" She ran into the kitchen and showed them her ring. They made a face, "Don't tell me you guys already knew."

Jake walked into the room, "Come on babe I'm old school. I asked for their permission and they said yes."

"I can't believe this is happening." Olivia couldn't wipe the smile off her face. She hugged her parents and ran into the room where her kids were.

"Look Lea, look Elijah, look what mommy got from Jake."

Lea looked at the ring, "Pretty," and she went back to what she was doing.

"We're moving today little ones."

Lea walked over to her, "Yeah we're going to live with Jake, right mommy?"

"That's right Lea, how do you feel about that?"

"Excited," was all she said. She hugged her babies tightly. She got them ready for the day; she fed them, and changed them. Olivia thought to herself, "This is the best day of my life."

Thirty-five

Olivia, her parents, and Jake were all ready to start packing everything up into the truck. The kids were both in their playpens. When everything was packed up, they carried the babies to the car and buckled them in their car seats. Olivia kissed her parents,

"Thank you so much for your help today, I'll see you soon."

Her mom hugged her, "I know, now we have a wedding to plan."

"I know can you believe it?" Olivia hugged her dad and kissed him. She walked to the car and got in and buckled up. Jake drove the truck to the house and Olivia was going to meet them there.

When Olivia arrived at the house, there were a bunch of people at the house. She pulled up and got out of the car when everyone yelled,

"Congratulations!" She was grinning from ear to ear. Jake came over and gave her a big hug and he helped take the kids out.

"I can't believe you did this," she smiled at him.

"I love you Liv, I want to do everything in my power to make you happy."

She looked him in his eyes, "You do Jake."

"Okay then let's celebrate." They laughed and held on to the kids and walked into the house. Everyone helped moving the furniture into the house. Olivia was told to stay in the house and to tell everyone where everything was to go. She didn't mind that job. When the celebration came to an end, she put the kids to bed. When she walked out to the living room, Jake was sitting there waiting for her. He held out his arms out to her and she fell into them.

"This has been the best day by far Jake, thank you so much."

"No baby, thank you." She leaned back and kissed him, passionately. Jake started to rub his fingers through her hair and started to caress her shoulders.

Olivia was breathless, "Take me to bed Jake." He picked her up and took her to the bedroom. He laid her gently on the bed. He climbed in next to her kissing her slowly. She pulled his shirt off and kissed his chest and he was starting to groan. She unbuckled his pants and slid her hand down. She slid his pants down with his briefs. Jake started to breath heavy and moan. He pulled her back up and removed her shirt. He took off her bra and he kissed and caressed her chest, she felt amazing. He slid off her pants and spread her legs and started going down on her. She was moaning in ecstasy calling his name.

"I want you so much Jake, I love you."

"I love you Liv." Jake came back up, he started to reach for a condom and she stopped him. "Are you sure?" She shook her head, at that moment Jake never saw her look more beautiful. He took her in his arms and put himself inside her. At first she was uneasy but then she relaxed immediately. He turned her around and she was on her stomach and he put it inside her. She was trying not to be loud but it felt amazing. He was so deep inside her. She pulled him off of her so she could be on top of him. He reached up and felt her chest in his hands; she got even more turned on. He climaxed inside of her and moaned in ecstasy. They fell asleep entwined in each other.

When she woke up the next morning, Jake was still sleeping. She knew she had a big day to unpack everything. She checked on the kids and saw they were awake.

"Mommy," cried Lea.

"Good morning Lea." She picked her up and kissed her and put her down. She walked over to Elijah and picked him up, he smiled at her. "Did you sleep okay?" They both shook their heads. "Are you ready to eat?" She walked them into the kitchen, put them in their high chairs and looked in the fridge for the food she put in there last night. She prepared the food and gave it to them. She walked over to the coffee maker and made a pot. Just as it was finishing, Jake walked in the kitchen.

"Morning beautiful," he kissed her. "Morning little ones," he walked over and kissed Lea and Elijah. "I smelled the coffee all the way from the bedroom." She laughed and went to the cabinet and grabbed two mugs. "So what do you want to do today?"

She poured the coffee, "I'm going to unpack."

He walked up behind her, "Do whatever you want to do to this house, it's yours now too."

She turned around and kissed him, "Thank you Jake." She made some breakfast for her and Jake and they ate together with the kids at the table. When they were finished, she took the kids, gave them their baths and dressed them. She put the playpens into the living room so she can watch them while she was unpacking.

By dinnertime, she was done setting everything up the way she wanted. They decided to make it a pizza night. It was getting late and Olivia was exhausted. She put the kids to sleep and finally plopped down on the couch. Jake came from the kitchen and sat down next to her.

"Hey there baby, how you doing?"

She looked at him sleepily, "I'm tired." He scooped her up and took her to bed.

"Sweet dreams baby." Olivia passed out immediately. She woke up with a startle in the middle of the night to someone touching her; she didn't know where she was at first. She suddenly realized she was home now with Jake and he was caressing her, she lay there half asleep. He climbed on top of her and pulled her panties down and put himself inside her and she started to moan. She never experienced lovemaking but she knew that this is what it was to the fullest. Jake was moving quicker and quicker and he was groaning louder and then he finished inside her," I love you Olivia," and kissed her. Olivia smiled and kissed him back, she felt blissfully happy.

Thirty-six

*W*eeks later, Olivia woke up and lay there with Jake and he was staring at her.

"What are you looking at?" she smiled.

"You're just so beautiful Liv." She blushed.

"You're not so bad yourself." All of a sudden she got a familiar feeling in her stomach and ran to the bathroom.

Jake ran after her, "You okay babe? Do you have the stomach virus?"

Olivia looked up at him, "I think I'm pregnant."

Jake had a huge smile on his face, "Are you sure?"

"I have to take a test to be sure but I think that I am." He went over to her and hugged her. It will be okay Liv, I'm here for you. "Thank God for that." She went to the cabinet and pulled out a pregnancy test and decided to take it.

"Where did you get the test from?" Jake asked.

"Last time I went to the grocery store I saw them and decided to get them. I don't know just in case this happened."

"I guess it's a good thing you got them then," he smiled.

"Are you going to stand here and watch me take it," she laughed.

"I'll wait outside the bathroom; let me know when you're done." When she finished she called him inside the bathroom. "What do we do now?"

"We just wait," she smiled. A minute later she saw the 2 lines and she knew. "It looks like we're having a baby."

He picked her up, kissed and hugged her, "Oh my God Liv, I can't believe it, now we have to get married right away."

"Good thinking."

"How are you feeling now?"

"I'm feeling okay now."

"Good." He took her hand and led her back to the bedroom and undressed her. "You're so beautiful, especially now with a baby inside you." He laid her down on the bed and kissed her gently. He kissed her stomach and then her chest. He kissed and caressed each one. He took her by the mouth and kissed her, "I love you so much Liv." She climbed on top of him and slid herself down onto him and they both moaned in ecstasy. When they were done they lay there holding each other.

"I can do this the right way and go to the doctor for this pregnancy." He smiled at her and touched her belly. Olivia got up and went to the kid's room and they were up. Lea was walking around the room and Elijah was just sitting on the carpet. "What are you two doing out of your cribs?" She picked each one up and took them to the bath and then she changed and fed them. She called her doctor to make an appointment to make sure she was pregnant. She was able to get an appointment that day.

She got on the phone with her parents, "Hey mom I was wondering if you could come over and watch the kids for us, or we could drop them off to you."

"Oh honey we'll come to you it's no problem." She told them when to come and hung up the phone.

Jake was in the kitchen making coffee and she turned to him, "I don't think we should tell my parents yet, not until we know for sure."

"Sounds like a plan, we can surprise them."

"You're going to come with me, I hope."

"Of course I am baby." When her parents arrived they kissed the kids goodbye and left. When they arrived to the doctors they were both pretty nervous. They sat in the waiting room holding hands. When her name was called they got up and went to the room to see the doctor. She had to change into a gown and they asked her a ton of questions. The nurse left the room and they waited for the doctor to come.

"Are you doing alright, Liv?"

"Yeah I'm just nervous."

Just then the doctor came in, "Hello there Olivia, how are you? What can I help you with today?"

"I'm doing okay; I think that I'm pregnant."

The doctor looked at Jake, "Are you the father?"

Jake smiled nervously, "Yes, yes I am." The doctor looked back at Olivia; do you have any other children?"

"I actually have two other kids, which is a long story."

"Are they from you Jake?"

"No ma'am." Olivia looked at the doctor; "I was raped by the same man for a couple years and ended up having two children."

"Oh Olivia I'm so sorry."

"It's okay Jake's here now."

"Okay well let's take a look." She did a thorough exam, "Congratulations you two but I was wondering if twins run in either of your families?"

"Not that I know of, how about you Jake?" Olivia asked.

"Not that I know of, why?"

"Well it looks like you're having not one baby but two babies." Olivia looked shocked but happy and looked at Jake; he also looked shocked. "You're about eight weeks along and it's very important you take good care of them right now more than ever."

"Yes of course, thank you doctor." The doctor wrote a prescription for vitamins and they left.

When they got home the kids were playing with their toys and her parents were watching them in the living room.

"Hey you two, is everything alright?"

Olivia smiled at Jake, "We have something we want to tell you." Her parents looked at both of them, suspiciously.

"Well what is it?" asked her mom.

"I'm pregnant mom and dad, with twins." Her mom and dad jumped up and hugged her and hugged Jake.

"That's great sweetie! I'm so happy for you, so happy for both of you. How are you feeling?"

"I feel okay, just a little tired. It looks like we need to move the wedding up closer than we thought."

"Of course sweetie, what do you think about a backyard wedding?"

Olivia smiled, "Actually that would be perfect. How do you feel about that Jake?"

"I'm perfectly happy with whatever you want to do Liv."

A few weeks later, the wedding was here. They decided to have it in their backyard with close friends and family. The day was perfect and it couldn't have gone any better. The kids were a part of the wedding and they had a blast. Olivia and Jake were so happy to have everyone there to enjoy in their special day. When it was all over and everyone went home, they plopped down on the couch and fell asleep with the kids laying on them.

The next morning, they prepared to go away for their honeymoon. Olivia hated to leave her kids for a week but her mom convinced her that she needed to get away. They hopped on a plane to the Caribbean. Olivia finally felt relaxed and she basked in the sun. It was finally nice to have alone time with Jake.

When they got back home, Olivia looked at her kids and swore they have grown. She kissed her mom and dad and gave them little gifts for helping them out. She kissed her kids and gave them some gifts as well. She was finally ready to start her life with her kids, the babies inside her and Jake.

Two months had passed and Olivia and Jake were looking forward to meeting their new babies. Olivia felt like life was going the way she finally wanted. Her children were growing so fast and they were chatting away and walking. Lea was now four and Elijah was three. They were excited to have little brothers or sisters. Olivia was getting ready to go to the appointment to find out the sex of the baby. She was going alone because Jake was working and her parents were babysitting the kids. When she got to the doctor she waited patiently. She realized she was about four months pregnant now and she was excited.

"Olivia Mallor." Olivia looked up and got up, the nurse smiled at her, "How are you feeling?"

"I'm good I'm just a little tired, and its Harrison now."

"That's wonderful, congratulations!"

"Thank you!" They walked down the hallway and into the exam room; the nurse took her blood pressure and weighed her. She gave her the gown to change in to and told her the doctor would be in shortly. Olivia changed quickly and sat on the table waiting for her to come in.

There was a knock on the door, "Come in." In came Dr. Judy.

"Hey there Olivia, how are you feeling?"

"I'm feeling pretty good today, just been kind of tired."

"That's normal. No Jake today?"

"Unfortunately he had to work today."

She smiled, "Of course. Okay let's get started, lay back for me." Olivia did what she was told. The doctor started the ultrasound, "Are you excited to find out the sex of the babies?"

"Yes very excited!"

The doctor was looking at the ultrasound, "It looks like the twins are doing very well."

"Can you tell what the sex is?"

"Let me take a look." It took her a few minutes but she finally turned to her. "It looks like you're going to have a boy and a girl." Olivia put her hand to her mouth tears came to her eyes.

"Thank you so much doctor."

"Now Olivia you must take it easy now because this is a critical time. With twins they sometimes want to come a lot sooner, so please try and take it easy and rest. You can get dressed now and I'll see you after." When the doctor left Olivia felt so elated, she got dressed and went out to meet her. She gave her some pamphlets and she spoke to her about the twins and told her that she and the babies were doing great. Olivia thanked the doctor and left the office.

When she got out to the car, she was so thrilled. She pulled out her cell phone and decided to ring Jake but he didn't answer. She left him a sweet message but didn't want to reveal the sex of the babies.

On her way home she decided to take a different way home. She found herself looking at the pretty scenery; she didn't notice a car coming up behind her. In one brief moment everything turned into a disaster. The car came up behind her and struck her hard. Her car slanted and veered to the center of the road. It did a full 360 before it stopped and Olivia's world turned black.

Thirty-seven

When Olivia woke up, she realized she was in the back of a car. Whose car, she didn't know. She looked up and saw a woman driving the car.

"Well hello there, sunshine."

"S…Sarah, is that you?"

"Who did you expect?"

"What are you doing here?" Olivia started to cry and scream.

Sarah pulled over, "No need to do that Liv, after all you don't want me to hurt you and the precious baby you have in your belly do you?" Olivia just shook her head with tears streaming down her face. She couldn't believe that this was happening to her. "He is going to be so happy to see you and with another one on the way," Sarah laughed. She pulled off and away they went. Wherever they went it took about an hour to get there.

Sarah pulled into the driveway and turned off the ignition. She got out of the car and opened the back door and pulled Olivia out.

"Where are we?"

Sarah smiled at her, "You'll see soon enough." They walked up the steps to the house. All around them were trees. It was secluded in the middle of nowhere. Sarah knocked twice and the door opened. There was Chris staring right at her. Olivia screamed and tried to run but Sarah grabbed her in time. They took her in the house and shut the door.

"Well well, there is my pudding, and it looks like you're with child. How are you doing Liv?"

"How did you find me? What are you doing here? How did you get out of jail?"

Chris looked at her and walked around her, "You ask too many questions," and he slapped her in the face. Olivia winced in pain and grabbed the side of her face. "You hurt me Liv, like really bad. You're going to pay for your mistakes. How far along are you?"

Olivia looked scared, "Why?"

He came up behind her and grabbed her stomach, "Because I want to know."

"I'm four months."

"Kind of big for four months, don't you think Liv?" She shook her head. "Come on let's take a walk." He grabbed her hand and walked down the hall. He opened up a door and there was Joy. Olivia gasped, Chris pushed her inside the room and shut the door and locked it.

"Oh my God, Joy what are you doing here?"

Joy looked like an awful mess, "They found me. I don't know how but they found me."

"How long have you been here?"

"I'm not sure but it feels like forever, maybe a couple weeks. It was like they scouted me out and found me. I guess they did the same to you?"

"I can't be here Joy. I need to get out of here, we both do."

"Well as you can see there are no windows and we can't get out of the door we came in from."

"I can't believe that this happening again."

"It is what it is but I see that you are carrying again. I'm assuming it's by Jake?"

Olivia shook her head, "We actually got married a few months ago." Joy just laughed and sat there. Olivia was about to say something when the door opened and in came Chris, Sarah was right behind him.

"Well hello you two it's nice to have you both back. Sarah has been kind enough to bring you both back to me where you will remain for a long, long time." He walked over to Olivia and picked up her hand, "I see you got married," and he dropped her hand back down. "Sarah, I want you to watch Joy for me for a minute. Take her into the living room; I need a moment here with Olivia." Sarah did what she was told and Chris walked over to the door and shut it. He walked over to Olivia and ran his hands through her hair and pulled her head back. He used his other hand and ripped her shirt off, Olivia started to scream. He pulled out a handkerchief out of his back pocket, "Don't make me use this." He pulled her pants off and she stood there naked and vulnerable. "I'm digging that belly on you Liv, just like old times. Now get your ass over by the wall."

"Please Chris I don't want to do this. Please don't hurt me or my babies?"

He looked at her for a minute, "Did you say babies?" Olivia regretted saying that. "Answer me!"

"Yes I said babies, I'm having twins."

"Wow," was all he could muster. "Turn around for me."

"But Chris I…" but before she could say anything he pushed her against the wall. She didn't want him to hurt her or the babies so she stood against the wall. She heard the familiar sound of him unbuttoning his pants, and she felt him put himself inside her. She wanted to scream but she couldn't. He pushed inside her and started to thrust hard into her.

"You missed this baby, didn't you? I could tell you're so wet." He grabbed her chest hard and she winced in pain. He covered her mouth and pounded her as tears were streaming down her face. When he was finished, he pushed her down like she was trash and walked out of the room. The door opened once more and Sarah pushed Joy inside. She saw how horrible Olivia looked and ran to her.

Olivia kept crying over and over again, "I thought this was over, my babies my poor babies." Joy was holding her close. "I need to get out of here Joy. I can't do this again I'm pregnant with Jake's babies.

"Did you say babies?"

Olivia tried to stop crying, "Yeah I'm carrying twins." They heard the door open once more and in came Sarah, carrying some food for them.

She plopped the tray down on the floor and started to walk out but Joy yelled to her, "How could you let him do this to us again? Especially with a pregnant, married woman? Aren't you his girlfriend? You don't mind him screwing other girls?" Sarah just looked at the both of them and stormed out of the room, locking the door behind her.

266

Sarah walked down the hallway to where Chris was laying on the couch, "So what's the deal with you Chris? I thought we were an item."

"We are babe, what makes you think otherwise?"

"I don't know maybe the fact maybe that you just raped Olivia."

Chris looked up at her, "Yeah well I have my reasons."

"Bullshit!" Sarah yelled. "I'm out of here," and she walked to the door.

"Where do you think you're going?"

"I'm not going to be with someone that screws other women."

"You'll do what I say Sarah."

"Don't talk to me like that and she started to walk towards the door when he pulled her back. He punched her hard in the face and she dropped to the ground. He picked her up and laid her on the couch. He didn't want to do that but he lost his temper.

When Sarah came too, she had a horrible headache. She saw Chris sitting next to her and she started to scream.

He covered her mouth, "I'm so sorry Sarah I didn't mean to do that to you. I didn't do anything with any of them since we've been together. I love you Sarah, please don't scream." He let go of her and she sat there looking at him.

"Do you promise you didn't do anything?"

"Of course I didn't do anything with them baby."

"Well they claimed that you did and you even said you did."

"And who are you going to believe, them or me? I was only kidding, I would never do that." Sarah looked at him and smiled and she grabbed him and kissed him. They took off each other's clothes off and he put himself inside her and exploded into her. Olivia and Joy could hear what was happening, they heard Sarah screaming one minute and the next they were having sex.

"I guess Sarah doesn't care that Chris has sex with other girls," said Joy.

When Sarah and Chris were finished, Sarah decided to take a walk into the back room where Olivia and Joy were. She opened the door and stood there staring at them.

Olivia looked at Joy and then at Sarah, "Something wrong Sarah?"

Sarah walked over to her and pushed her backwards, "Don't ever talk shit to me about my boyfriend." Olivia was standing against the wall.

Joy got up and got in Sarah's face, "What the hell are you talking about Sarah?"

"You lied and said she slept with Chris while I was in the other room."

"First off I didn't lie, he lied to you. Second of all he raped her; they didn't "sleep" together! Maybe you should get your facts straight before you go and accuse us. I think we've been through enough." Sarah just looked at her and didn't say anything; instead she turned around and left. "Are you doing alright Liv?"

"Yeah I'm okay. What the hell was that about?"

"I'm sure Chris lied to her and said he didn't touch you. Did you see her eye? It looks like she got it good."

Olivia slid down the wall and held her belly, "We need to get out of here Joy. Maybe we can convince Sarah to turn on Chris."

"It doesn't hurt to try."

Thirty-eight

Olivia and Joy lay on the floor of the room they were held in. It was cold, dirty, and damp. The door suddenly opened and in came Chris. He saw them lying on the floor huddled next to each other. He bent down and pulled Joy up by her hair and she screamed bloody murder but he punched her in the face and stomach and she fell to the floor, knocked her unconscious. Olivia looked deathly afraid, she quickly covered her stomach.

"Don't worry baby I won't hurt you, I just don't like people saying shit about me to Sarah." He knelt down over her, "How are you feeling today?" He put his hands through her hair and worked his way down to her chest and then felt her belly and went down to her crotch.

Olivia just shook in fear, "Please stop, Chris." He stopped what he was doing to her and made a fist at her and jerked back but didn't do anything. He stood up and he walked out the door. Olivia scrambled over to Joy, "Joy, can you hear me, Joy?" She stroked her hair and rocked her back and forth.

Joy started to come out of it, "What, what happened?"

"Oh Joy, I thought you were gone," Olivia cried. "Chris came in and did a number on you." Joy tried to get up but her head was killing her and she lay back down. "Did he do anything to you, are you alright?"

"I'm fine, he didn't touch me. I'm so sorry this is happening again Joy. I know it destroyed you."

Joy looked up, "It's not your fault Liv so don't ever think that."

"I know but you moved away to get away from him and he still found you." Joy just lay there not saying anything. Olivia was right they had to get out of there; otherwise they were going to break.

Sarah came in and dropped off the food and saw Joy's face.

"I guess someone might stop telling lies now," Sarah snickered and left. I can't believe she thinks we're lying. Why the hell would we lie about something like that?" said Joy.

"He really got into her head, I don't know how we're going to convince her," said Olivia.

Two months had passed and Olivia and Joy were still being held hostage. Chris would sneak in and repeatedly raped Joy while Sarah was sleeping.

That morning, Joy woke up not feeling well. Olivia was a lot bigger and she was now about six months pregnant. She rolled over and saw Joy in the corner throwing up into the trashcan.

"You okay Joy?"

Joy went back to where Olivia was laying and settled next to her, "I hope to God I'm not pregnant but I think I am." Olivia frowned. "I don't think I can handle this again Liv," she cried.

When Chris came in, he dropped off the food and saw them laying there on the floor, "Good morning ladies."

Joy looked at him, "I need a pregnancy test." Chris smiled at her and pulled one out of his pocket. He picked her up and took her out to the bathroom and told her to pee.

When they got the results, he smiled even wider, "Congratulations mommy." He took her back into the room, "Take care of that baby for me," and he walked out the door.

Olivia looked at Joy, "Positive," said Joy. She sat down on the floor and just started crying, "Why is this happening to us? What did we do to ever deserve this?"

"It's not our fault Joy, we can't help that he's a psycho. We didn't know that when we met him, but we have to stay strong now, not only for ourselves but for our babies as well."

"I know I'm trying but I can't believe that sadistic psycho carries pregnancy tests!" Sarah walked in the door and they saw a swell in her stomach, "Are you pregnant?" asked Olivia.

"Well if you must know, yes I am," Sarah beamed.

"Well in case you didn't know, Joy is also pregnant."

"What do you mean you're pregnant? Were you pregnant when you got here?"

"News flash Sarah, we told you that Chris was raping us and you didn't believe us!"

Sarah looked mortified, "Are you sure you weren't pregnant before you came here?"

Joy looked at her with crazy eyes, "Are you serious right now Sarah?"

Olivia stood up, "We have to get this creep Sarah, please help us!" Sarah didn't say anything; it was like she was thinking about something. All of a sudden she turned around and walked out of the room.

"Well that went well," cried Joy. All of a sudden they heard a bunch of commotion coming from outside the door. The door opened and Chris pushed Sarah inside and slammed the door and locked it. She was hysterically crying. Olivia gave Joy a look that puzzled her; she got up and went to her.

"Sarah, are you alright?" Sarah was trying to say something but her sobbing made it impossible to make out what she was saying. Olivia knelt down next to her and Joy walked over to her and knelt down on the other side of her.

"It's okay Sarah, we're here for you," said Joy.

She looked up at her and then at Olivia, "You don't hate me?"

Olivia and Joy looked at each other, "Of course not Sarah, "said Olivia. Sarah felt relieved and turned to Olivia and hugged her. Sarah hugging her took Olivia aback. She sat there and let her hug her. "Sarah, what happened?" Sarah removed herself from Olivia and started to calm down.

"After I left the room, I went in and spoke to Chris about Joy's pregnancy. One minute he was fine telling me one thing and the next it was like he went crazy. The stories he was giving me I could tell were bullshit so I called him out on it. He got pissed off and he grabbed me and threw me in here with you guys. I'm so sorry I didn't believe you guys, I hope you can forgive me."

Joy and Olivia walked over to her and hugged her, "Of course we forgive you."

They let go of each other, "We have to figure out a way out of here," said Olivia.

"If Chris comes in, maybe I can try and make nice with him again. I can act like I want him and that he's telling the truth," said Sarah.

"I don't know Sarah, are you sure you would want to do that?"

"I owe it to the both of you to try." Joy and Olivia looked at each other and then they looked at Sarah, "Are you sure?"

"Yes, I have to do this." Just then the door opened and in came Chris with some food. He set it down and he started walking toward the door. Sarah looked at Olivia and at Joy and she stood up, "Chris wait," Sarah said. He turned around and gave her look, "Please take me with you I don't want to be in here with these bitches. They're liars. I believe you and I just want to be with you." He looked at her and he grabbed her and kissed her hard. He held out his hand and opened the door, she quickly winked at Olivia and Joy and they left the room.

Chris took Sarah into the back bedroom and took her clothes off, "You mean whatcha said baby?"

"Of course I did Chris." He threw her down on the bed and had his way with her.

When he finally fell asleep; she snuck out of the room and into the living room. She saw the key to the room and grabbed it and started to walk to the back room. She then saw Chris heading to the bathroom and quickly put the key back and sat on the couch.

"What are you doing out here?"

"Oh I wasn't feeling that great so I came out here. I didn't want to disturb you."

He came up to her and cuddled up to her, "You feel alright now?"

"Yeah a little bit." He reached over to her belly and rubbed it. Sarah felt uneasy but she let him.

"I feel kind of hungry Chris and I'm craving a tuna hoagie, is it possible to get that?"

"You know the rules baby."

She looked at him with a sad face, "Please," she said.

He smiled at her, "Fine, but you have to stay here and watch them. I'll try and find a place that is low key." He grabbed the keys, kissed her goodbye and left. She watched the car pulled out of the driveway. She hurriedly grabbed the key to the room and unlocked it.

"Come on let's go!"

"Where's Chris?" said Olivia.

"I asked him to get me something to eat so he should be gone awhile." They walked through the door and down the hallway. Sarah peeked out the window just to make sure Chris was gone. They opened the door and walked out of the house.

They started down the driveway, "I think we should walk through the woods just in case Chris sees us," said Olivia.

"Good idea," said Joy. They started walking through the woods away from the house; they walked for what they felt was an eternity. They had no idea what time it was but they realized it was getting dark and it was starting to drizzle. "We need to take shelter. It's starting to rain heavier and pretty soon we won't be able to see what's in front of us," said Joy.

"What's that over there?" asked Sarah. They walked over and saw a little cove that could be used for shelter.

"Alright this looks like a good place to stay for the night," said Olivia.

"Do you think he's looking for us?" asked Joy.

"Of course he is, he thinks we're his property," said Olivia. They sat there for a while, "I think one of us should take watch for awhile and then we'll take turns." Sarah announced she would take the first watch. They sat there talking for a while until they were tired out and fell asleep.

Thirty-nine

Sarah jerked awake to a noise. It sounded like someone or something walking on leaves. She looked around but couldn't see anything it was just too dark. She looked over at Olivia and Joy but they were sleeping.

She tried waking them up, Joy stirred, "What's wrong Sarah?" she asked sleepily.

"I think there's someone out there."

Joy jerked more awake and heard snapping of a twig, "Shit, do you think we should wake up Liv?" Joy made up her mind and quietly woke up Olivia. "I think someone is out there." They sat there huddled together; not knowing what to do and they were scared to death. They didn't see any flashlights so they weren't sure what was making that noise. They heard footsteps coming closer and closer and then they just stopped. The girls sat there frozen, they didn't speak and they didn't breathe. All of a sudden they saw a deer walk by. They all took a sigh of relief and the deer ran off.

"That scared the hell out of me," said Sarah.

"I think that scared all of us," laughed Olivia. Before they knew it they fell asleep again and it was morning.

They woke up and they decided to set off. Olivia was so big and walking was the last thing she wanted to do but she had to. They came to a crossing where a little bridge was and they crossed over it. They saw someone ahead and they hid.

"Do you think that's him?"

"It's hard to tell." They watched him for a while but they couldn't tell if it was him so they kept on walking but away from the man. They ended up by a stream and they decided to wash up and get some water.

They got ready to head out again when the man appeared out of nowhere, "Are you girls lost?"

Sarah ran up to him, "Oh thank God! We've been kidnapped and we escaped. Can you please help us?" He looked at each one of the girls and saw Olivia was hugely pregnant.

"Come on my cabin is just down the road there." The girls got up and followed the man back to his cabin. They walked in and a woman was waiting for him, it was his wife. "Meredith, I found these girls out there in the woods."

She looked them over, "Oh my, what happened?"

Olivia walked forward, "We were kidnapped and held captive. Do you mind if we use your phone?"

"Of course my dear, are you all hungry?"

"Yes very."

"The phone is in there." The woman wrote the address down for her. Olivia walked over to the phone and dialed 911. She called Jake but she thought he sounded a little strange. He was elated to hear from her. He was on his way along with the police. The woman made them some soup and sandwiches and they gobbled them up quickly. "So, how far along are you?" asked the woman.

"Well I project between six and seven months now."

"Not too far to go then. Do you know what you're having?"

"I'm actually having twins, a boy and a girl."

"Twins, wow, congratulations!"

"Thank you." They all sat there in silence, "May we use the bathroom?" asked Olivia.

"All of you?"

"Well yeah, we are just used to being together all the time. We just feel safer this way."

"Sure, it's down the hall to the right." They all got up and headed to the bathroom. Once they were in there, Olivia locked the door.

"What's going on Liv? We never go to the bathroom together," said Joy.

"I just have an awful feeling something isn't right. I mean doesn't it seem odd that that man came out of nowhere? I think we should get out of here."

"Liv are you sure? They seem really nice and helpful; didn't you call the police and Jake?"

"Yeah I did, but it seemed a little weird and Jake didn't really sound like Jake. It almost seemed like the man was looking for us."

All of a sudden there was a knock on the door, "Is everything alright in there?" asked the woman.

"Uh yes, we'll be right out." There was a window in the bathroom and Olivia lifted the window, "Come on we'll get out this way." Joy and Sarah made it through the window. Olivia decided to run the sink water and then she climbed through the window. She was able to make it through and the girls helped her get down. Once they were all out of the window, they made a run for it down the side of the house. Just then a car pulled up and they hid behind a tree. It was Chris with a big old smile on his face. "See I knew something wasn't right," whispered Olivia.

"We have to leave now!" They started running through the woods and then they heard Chris yelling. He started running after them. They saw the stream and crossed over the bridge. They turned around to see if Chris was still there but they didn't see him. They saw the road up ahead; they hoped they could flag a car down to get help. Olivia saw a car approaching quickly. Sarah ran out to the road to flag it down and she realized as it was getting closer that it looked like Chris' car. She tried to jump out of the way of the car but he caught her and she tumbled backward to the edge of the road. Olivia ran over to her and she was just laying there knocked out cold.

Chris got out of the car, "Perfect! Look what you made me do?" He ran over to Sarah and put his arms around her. "Get in the fucking car!" he yelled to Olivia and Joy. He picked up Sarah and put her in the back of the car. Olivia and Joy started to take off. He got in the car and hunted them down and they went back into the woods to the cove where they can hide.

When they finally made it to the cove they sat there hidden. They heard him coming and they quietly sat there holding their breath. He walked by the cove and yelled, "Where are you bitches!" He went back to the car and took off.

The girls finally breathed, "I think he's gone, do you think Sarah will be okay?"

"I hope so; she was breathing when I checked her. Joy I don't know if I can run anymore, I feel like I'm going to pop any minute now."

"I know Liv; we have to figure out how to get out of here. I feel like we can't trust anyone now." They sat there for a while contemplating what to do.

"I don't understand those phone calls I made from that house; they must've been wired to Chris' house automatically."

"What are we going to do about Sarah?" asked Joy.

"I hate to say it, but we might have to go back to the house. We need to rescue her and take that car. I think it's the only way we'll be able to get out of here." Joy didn't seem too pleased to hear that but she didn't argue with her. They got up out of the cove and looked around and didn't see him. They started trekking through the woods back to the house.

When they made it back they decided to wait until the sun went down. They looked for things that could be used for weapons against Chris. When night approached, they looked through one of the windows and saw Chris wiping down Sarah. It looked like she wasn't moving.

He peeled off her clothes and his own clothes and he propped her up on the couch, "What in the hell is he doing?" whispered Joy.

"Doing what he does best, being a psycho." He lifted her legs and put them on his shoulders and he slipped himself inside her. He started thrusting himself and Sarah just lay there. "This is just sickening, I can't even watch," said Olivia. When he was done, he picked Sarah up and took her into the bedroom.

Forty

Olivia and Joy walked around the house to see if they could peer in the windows to see if they could see Chris and Sarah. The first window they came to, it appeared to be the bathroom and then they walked a little further down and came to another window. They peered through the glass and it was the bedroom. Chris and Sarah were lying in bed and it looked like Chris was sleeping.

They stepped away from the window, Olivia whispered to Joy, "I think we should go back to the front of the house and try the door." When they walked to the front of the house they tried the front door and it wouldn't open, he locked it. "Alright let's try the back door." They walked quietly to the back of the house and they tried the back door and it opened. They walked through the door very quietly. When they tried to shut the door it made a squeaky sound. Joy looked at Olivia and whispered, "Shit." It was so dark in the house that they couldn't see where they were going. They realized they came to the kitchen and stepped inside.

"Joy, try to find something to use as a weapon," Olivia whispered. They started searching the drawers and the cabinets. Olivia found a bottle opener and Joy only found a screwdriver. They walked out of the kitchen and started down the hallway. They noticed a candle was lit in the living room; they grabbed it and continued walking towards the bedroom where Sarah and Chris were. They paused when they saw the two of them lying in the bed. Sarah still looked like she was unconscious or possibly dead and there was blood covering her legs. They looked at each other with a worried look; Olivia took Joy's hand and led her back to the living room.

"Liv, what are we going to do? How are we going to get Sarah out of there without waking up Chris?" Olivia looked at what they had to use against him and then she looked at Joy.

"I think we're going to have to kill him Joy."

Joy looked at her in surprise, "What do you mean Liv?"

"We have to get out of here Joy. We need to rescue Sarah and this may be the perfect opportunity because he's sleeping." Joy didn't really want to but she didn't really have a choice. She looked at Olivia and shook her head yes. "Give me the screw driver. I have an idea." Joy gave her the screwdriver and Olivia gave her the bottle opener.

They started walking towards the bedroom again, they peered in and they were still lying in the same position. Olivia gave the candle to Joy to hold on to and Olivia walked over to Chris' side of the bed. She lifted the screwdriver and plunged it right down into his chest over and over. Chris opened his eyes right away and started thrashing around. Olivia ran to the other side of the bed. Joy was in shock she just stood there. She didn't know what to do. Olivia started screaming her name but Joy just stood there staring. She grabbed the bottle opener and ran to the other side. Chris was still shaking around in the bed, coughing up blood. Olivia stood over him, "You're not even worth it." She ran to the other side and shook Joy, she finally snapped out of it. "Come on, help me with Sarah!" she yelled. They both grabbed Sarah and walked out of the bedroom and into the living room. Olivia saw Chris' keys on the coffee table and grabbed them. They hurried out the back door and around to the front of the house to get to the car. When they got to the front of the house, they looked over and saw Chris outside by the front door. He started charging at them but fell down the steps, "Here Joy take the keys, get Sarah in the car!" she screamed. Olivia walked over to Chris who was trying to grab at her. She took out from her back pocket the bottle opener. She stabbed him in his neck and watched him cough and gargle the blood. "Go to Hell Chris!" She turned around and got in the car and started it up. Joy was freaking out hysterically. "Joy its okay, he's gone and he's not coming back!" She took her in her arms and hugged her tightly. "We have to get to the hospital for Sarah."

They started driving down the road to the hospital when Olivia realized her water broke. "Oh crap! My water just broke."

Joy looked at her, "What do you mean you're water broke? You're not even due yet?"

"I know I'm not but I need you to drive and fast." They pulled off to the side of the road and Joy got out of the car and went around to the driver side. She opened the door and helped Olivia out and helped her to the passenger side. Sarah was still laying in the backseat. When Olivia got in the car she realized that the babies were coming fast. "Uh Joy, I don't think I'm going to make it to the hospital. These babies want to come out, like now!" Joy looked scared but they've been through this before.

"Do you want me to try to get to the hospital?"

Olivia screamed, "I won't make it there Joy!"

Joy stated cursing to herself, "Okay Liv we'll have to deliver right here then." Olivia scooted herself in the middle of the front seat. Joy bent down and she saw baby number one coming quickly. She pulled off her jacket and helped get baby number one out safely. "It's a boy Liv," she wrapped the baby up in her jacket and placed the baby on the seat to prepare for the next baby. "You're doing great Liv hang in there. I see the next one." Olivia started pushing and screamed out. Joy delivered baby number two, "It's a girl." She wrapped her in a t-shirt that was lying on the floor of the car. "Are you okay Liv?" Olivia lay on the seat lifeless. Joy started shaking her but there was no response. She needed to get to the hospital for her and for the babies. She made sure the babies were nice and snug in the car and drove as fast as she could to the nearest hospital but the problem was she had no idea where she was. Finally she saw signs and followed them. When she made it to the hospital she pulled up to the emergency room doors and ran inside to fetch help. Out came doctors and nurses. They took the babies first and rushed them to the NICU and then they pulled Sarah out and then Olivia.

*F*orty-one

*J*oy needed to use the phone so she walked over to the pay phone and called Olivia's parents to let them know they were at the hospital and asked if they could get a hold of Jake. They obliged and they were on their way. She called her Uncle to let him know where she was and that she was safe. After she made the phone calls she sat down in the waiting room. A little while later a doctor came out and gave her some updates.

"Ms. Monroe," Joy stood up. "The babies are doing very well. Olivia did lose a lot of blood so we had to give her a transfusion but she will be fine, she's in recovery. As for Sarah, I'm sorry but she didn't make it." Joy felt relieved that the babies were doing okay and Olivia was going to make it but felt sad for the loss of Sarah.

"Thank you doctor, may I see Olivia yet?"

"She's resting right now but you can in a little while. Are you feeling all right, you look a little pale. I think we should check you out too." She took Joy in the back to one of the rooms to make sure she and the baby were okay. After the exam they determined that she was doing okay. There was a knock at the door and Jake was in the doorway.

"Jake, did you see Olivia?"

"Not yet, they wouldn't let me see her yet so I figured I would check on you."

"Did you see the babies?"

"Yeah I just came from seeing them; they're beautiful. Thank you Joy for your help, I really appreciate you taking care of her and delivering the babies safely. What happened?"

"It's a really long story. They found me in Oklahoma, kidnapped me and took me to the house and they followed Liv to the doctors. When she left there, Sarah veered her off the road and she got into an accident. She was fine but she took her. How are the kids holding up?"

"They're doing okay but they missed their mom."

"I'm glad they're doing okay." Joy looked up at Jake, "I just wanted to let you know that Sarah helped us escape. She turned on Chris."

"I'm grateful she did but it doesn't change the fact that she took my wife."

"Well you don't have to worry about them anymore Jake, they're both gone."

"Wait Chris is dead?"

"Yeah Olivia killed him. That's how we were able to get out of there and take the car."

Jake looked shocked and he sat down in the chair, "I had no idea she was capable of that."

"She saved my life Jake." There was a knock on the door and it was the doctor. Olivia is asking for you Jake.

He got up, "I'll tell her you were asking about her Joy."

"Thanks I'll see her later."

Jake walked out of the room and down the hall to Olivia's room. When he walked in, he walked up to her and kissed her forehead.

"Hey baby," he said.

"Jake, I'm so happy to see you." She took his hand in hers. "How are you? Are the kids alright?"

"Yeah they're fine Liv and I'm fine."

"How are the babies doing, are they alright? I don't really remember what happened."

"The babies are doing just fine, they're healthy."

"Oh thank goodness."

"I heard what you did Liv, with Chris I mean. You killed him."

"I had to do what I had to do to get out of that house Jake, I had no choice."

"I know baby, I just hope you're alright."

"I'm doing fine Jake; he's not going to hurt me or Joy ever again. How is Joy?"

"She's fine; I just saw her right before I came in here."

"How about Sarah, have you heard anything?"

"I'm sorry Liv, she didn't make it."

Olivia didn't look surprised, "I had a feeling." "Where are the kids? I would like to see them."

"Your parents have them; they should be here any minute."

"Can I see the babies?"

"They're in the NICU; I can wheel you to them."

"Do you mind?"

"Of course not babe let's go see them." He went to the nurses' station and asked them for a wheel chair to wheel her to see her newborns. When they got there, Olivia thought they looked so small.

"Since they were born prematurely, we had to put the babies in incubators but they're doing great," said the nurse. "Did you name them yet?"

Olivia looked at Jake, "We discussed it at one point but we've never decided."

"I think we have Liv."

"Are you sure?" Jake shook his head and smiled. "She will be Emma Rose and he will be Jake Charles Jr."

The nurse smiled, "They're great names."

Olivia looked at Jake and smiled, "Thank you."

After awhile they went back to her room and she got back in bed and lay down. There was a knock at the door and it was the kids and her parents.

"Mommy," they screamed. They both ran to her and gave her a hug and kiss. "We missed you mommy," said Lea.

"I've missed both of you very much. I'll be better soon. Do you want to meet your baby brother and sister?"

Lea's eyes lit up, "Yes please, can we go see them?"

"Jake will take you; I want to talk to Gigi and Grandpa." Jake took Lea and Elijah's hands and walked out of the room.

Her parents went to her and each kissed and hugged her, "We're so glad you're alright. We were so worried about you."

"I'm okay now, Chris is gone and for good this time."

"I know sweetheart, Jake told us. That was a very brave thing you did." Olivia lay there and she was feeling tired, "We'll let you get some rest and we'll come back later." Olivia shook her head and closed her eyes.

When she woke up the next morning, she looked over and she saw Jake sleeping on the chair.

The nurse came in and checked her, "How are you feeling this morning Olivia?"

"I'm feeling okay, maybe a little hungry."

"That's a good sign. I'll get you some breakfast," and she left.

"Hey," said Jake.

"Hey there," Liv said.

He got up from the chair and kissed her, "How are you feeling?"

"I'm feeling a little better."

"That's great babe."

"Where are the kids?"

"Your parents took them, they'll be back later."

The nurse came in with a tray of food, "Eat up now so you can get your strength," she smiled as she walked out of the room. Olivia ate her food and felt a lot better.

"I want to see Emma and JR."

Jake looked at her and laughed, "JR?"

"Yeah I want to call him JR," she grinned.

"If that's what you want to call him babe that's fine with me," Jake said.

The day arrived when Olivia could go home. The kids were with Jake when he picked her up. She was so excited to see them but she was sad to leave her babies behind but she knew that they would join her in a month. They had a lot of growing to do.

When Olivia got home, Jake had a surprise for her. He blindfolded her and led her down the hall to the bedroom.

"What is going on Jake?"

"You'll see baby." He took her hand and led her into the room. He took off her blindfold and she gasped. She looked around the room and it was perfect. There were two cribs on each side of the window. By the wall of the door was a changing station that was decorated with little lambs. There were two brown rocking chairs in the center of the room with a rug on top of the carpet with alphabet letters on it.

"This is amazing Jake, I can't believe you did this."

"I did it for us baby, I love you so much."

"I love you." She took him in his arms and hugged him tightly, "I'm so glad to be home."

The kids came into the room, "Did you see what we did mommy?"

"Yes it's perfect, thank you all so much." She leaned down and hugged Lea and Elijah tightly.

Mommy, when do Emma and JR come home?" asked Lea.

"They'll be here soon; they just have to get a little bigger and stronger."

*F*orty-two

A few months had passed and it was the day the babies were finally getting out of the hospital. Olivia was excited to finally have them home. They dropped Lea and Elijah off at their grandparents and went off to the hospital to pick up their babies. When they arrived they went right up to the nursery and they were all ready to be taken home. The nurses and doctors wished Olivia and Jake good luck and they left. The babies still looked so tiny. Olivia fixed the car seats to fit to their little bodies. She put them in the car seats and they drove home.

When they got home, Olivia and Jake took them to the new nursery. They both took turns holding them and they fed them and changed them. They laid them down in their cribs and they peacefully went to sleep. When Lea and Elijah got home, they wanted to see them.

"They're sleeping right now but when they wake up I'll take you to them. Right now it's bedtime," Olivia said. Lea just shook her head in disappointment.

Jake bent down, "Don't worry sweetie you will have a long time with them." Olivia took her and Elijah to wash up and get ready for bed. When they were all finished she put tucked them in their beds and read to them until they fell asleep. She went and checked in on the babies and saw Jake standing there.

"Are you okay Jake?"

He turned and smiled, "Yeah baby, I'm just watching them sleep." She took his hand and led him to the living room.

"Come on sit down and relax." They sat there on the couch for awhile, "I'm so happy Jake and I feel like life is finally complete. I have you and I have the kids, what else could I ask for?"

"I feel the same way baby and he kissed her deeply. Just then the baby monitor went off and they both got up and walked into the nursery. They were both crying so they picked them up and held them and sang to them. They finally started to calm down so Olivia and Jake prepared the bottles and gave it to them and they drank eagerly. They put them back in their cribs and went back into the living room,

"Welcome to babyhood Jake," she laughed. He tickled her and she laughed, "I think we should get ready for bed," he lifted her up and took her to the bedroom. They made love and fell asleep in each other's arms.

In the morning, Olivia woke up to hear voices coming from the baby monitor; she knew it was Lea and Elijah. She got up, went to the bathroom and went into the nursery.

"Hey what are you two doing in here," she smiled.

"We wanted to see them mommy."

"I know you both did but you have to wait until daddy or I are with you, okay?"

Just then Jake came in, "What's going on in here?"

"They wanted to see JR and Emma."

"Of course they did." The babies were stirring in their cribs, "I think we should take them out Liv." She went over and picked up Emma and he picked up JR. They each sat down at the rocking chairs and showed them their new baby brother and sister. Lea and Elijah were in awe.

"They're so small," said Lea.

"You were that small once Lea." Lea laughed. Elijah was more shy and stood there watching. "What do you think Elijah?"

"They're okay," was all he could say. They all just laughed.

Jake's cell phone started to ring, "Babe I have to get that." He placed JR in the crib and went into the bedroom to get his phone. Olivia sat in the chair rocking Emma and she heard Jake whisper a curse.

"Lea can you take your brother and go in the kitchen? I'm going to put Emma down and I'll be there in a minute to make you breakfast."

"Okay, come on Elijah." They left and went into the kitchen. Olivia put Emma down and walked down the hall to the bedroom and saw Jake sitting on the bed.

"What's wrong Jake? I heard you curse."

"I think you better sit down Liv." She could tell Jake wasn't kidding around and something was seriously wrong. "Do you remember Joe?"

"You mean Joe that helped Chris?"

He looked at her, "Yeah that's the one."

"What about him Jake, he's in jail, isn't he?"

He took her hand, "He was released yesterday Liv due to good behavior."

"Great! Maybe we should take the kids and go somewhere else or do you think we will be okay? I mean he has to be on some kind of…"

Jake cuts her off, "Liv, there's something else I have to tell you."

"Can it wait Jake? The kids are in the kitchen waiting for breakfast."

"No it can't."

"What's wrong? What is it Jake?" She started to feel a little panicked.

"It's Joy."

Olivia got up, "What do you mean its Joy, what happened to Joy?" She grabbed his phone and tried to dial her number. Jake took the phone, "Please Jake tell me she's okay," tears were starting to form and roll down her face.

"When Joe got out, he found out where she lived and he went there with the intention of killing her. He broke into her home and murdered her father and drowned Joy in the swimming pool. I'm so sorry Liv."

Olivia sat down screaming and crying, "What do you mean? Joy is dead?"

Just then Lea and Elijah came in, "Aunt Joy is dead," and they started crying. Olivia took them in her arms and held them. She didn't know what to do, she felt devastated.

"Jake what do we do?"

"We have to keep you and the children safe."

"They didn't find him, did they?"

"Unfortunately they're still looking for him."

"I think I should call my parents to warn them, let them know he's on the loose." She got on the phone and called her mom but there was no answer so she left a message. "That's weird, my mom didn't answer."

"I'm sure she's fine Liv."

"Jake I can't take that as an answer, especially with Joe out there."

"I know baby but I think it would be a good idea to just wait it out here." Just then the phone rang, it was Olivia's mom.

"Mom, are you and dad okay?"

"Yes Liv we're both fine, why is something wrong?"

"Joy is dead. Joe got out of jail and he killed her and he's out there somewhere. I just wanted to make sure he didn't come there."

"Oh no, I'm so sorry sweetie, are you alright?"

"I'm pretty upset but I'm glad you guys are alright. Can you please be safe and be aware of your surroundings?"

"Of course we will sweetheart." Olivia got off the phone with her parents and went into the kitchen to make her kids something to eat for breakfast.

"Babe I'm sorry but I have to go to work, they called me in."

"But Jake, after what just happened I'm afraid to be alone."

"Call your parents, they'll come by and help you with the kids."

"I guess I can do that."

"Hey don't be like that; I'll be home as soon as I can. I love you baby."

"I love you too," he kissed her and he left. She called her parents to come over so she didn't have to be alone and to help with the babies; they happily agreed to come over.

*F*orty-three

*W*hen her parents arrived Olivia was so glad to see them.

"I'm so happy you guys are okay, I can't believe Joy is gone. What about her kids, I feel so awful." Her mom walked over to her and hugged her tightly. "Maybe I should go and see her mom and the kids."

"Are you sure you want to do that Liv?" asked her dad.

"I feel like it's only right." Her mom smoothed her hair, "Well if you feel like you need to, then maybe you should."

"Thanks mom. I'll be home soon."

"Hey Liv, please be careful." Olivia shook her head. She kissed her kids and the babies and she left. She got in the car and drove off to see Joy's mother.

312

When she pulled up out front, she took a deep breath and walked up to the door and knocked. At first nobody answered but then she heard someone inside.

"Mrs. Monroe, its Olivia. Are you home?"

Then the door opened, "I'm sorry Olivia, I thought you were a reporter. They've been driving me crazy coming here, please come in." Olivia walked in and saw all the toys all around. "I'm sorry about all the mess, I wasn't really expecting anyone," as she sat down.

"Mrs. Monroe I'm really sorry about what happened, where are the kids?"

She waved toward the hallway, "They're napping."

"Have they asked about Joy?"

Her mom had tears in her eyes, "They ask about her all the time. I haven't had the heart to tell them yet. Hey maybe you can tell them.

"But they hardly know me."

Joy's mom got up and sat down next to Olivia, "They've been through a lot and you've been there with them for most of that, they know who you are."

Olivia started to cry, "I don't think it's my place to tell them but I do want to see them."

"Go ahead they're down there." Olivia got up, dried her tears and went down the hallway to where the kids were sleeping. She opened the door and walked in, she saw them lying on the bed. Their little chests were moving up and down. She went to the bed and sat down and caressed their heads.

Ethan woke up, "Mommy is that you?"

"Uh hello Ethan, I'm not sure if you remember me or not, but I'm Olivia."

He rubbed his eyes and realized, "I remember you," and he hugged her. "Hope wake up, its Olivia."

"Ethan you don't have to wake her." It was already too late, she woke up and rolled over and she looked sleepily over at Olivia. Olivia smiled at her.

Hope stood up and looked at her, "You're mommy's friend, is she here?"

Olivia looked at the both of them and frowned, "I'm sorry she's not here. I'm just here to visit."

"I want my mommy," cried Hope.

"I know you do but you're grandmother is here."

"We don't want her, she smells and she doesn't take care of us," said Ethan.

"What do you mean she doesn't take care of you?"

"We are always hungry and she doesn't change us or bathe us." Olivia started to look around the room and she noticed that it was a disaster. There were clothes, dirty plates and cups piled everywhere. She looked closely at the children and they looked filthy and they were awfully skinny.

"Okay kids come on, put your shoes on we're taking a little trip."

The kids hopped off the bed, "Where are we going?" yelled Ethan.

"We're going to go to my house; you can see Lea and Elijah. Do you remember them?"

"Sort of," he said.

"Okay well you can meet them again when we get there." They put their shoes on and she helped them get dressed. She grabbed their hands and walked back into the living room. Joy's mother was lying on the couch with what appeared to be a bottle of vodka next to her and she was passed out.

"What happened to grandma," asked Hope.

"She's tired and been through a lot. I'm going to write her a note to let her know I have you both." She put the note down next to her and took the kids hands and walked out of the house. She strapped them into the car seats and drove back to her house.

When she pulled up, she noticed Jake's car there. She got the kids out of the car and took them up to the house. When she opened the door, Jake was frantic.

"Liv, where have you been? Who are they?"

"I told my mom that I was going to visit Joy's kids and to see how her mom was doing."

"She did tell me that but I called your cell phone a hundred times and you didn't answer."

"Oh I left it in the car, sorry Jake."

"You had me worried sick."

"Well I'm home now and I brought Ethan and Hope Anne with me. Come on let's go see Elijah and Lea. I'll be right back Jake and we'll talk." She brought the kids to see them and at first they were unsure but then they remembered each other and started playing.

"Thanks mom and dad for watching them."

"It's okay, don't worry about it, I hope everything went okay." Olivia made a face and nodded to the kids.

She walked back to Jake and sat down, "Its Joy's mother. She's not taking care of them. They told me that she's not feeding them or bathing them. Did you see how thin they were?"

"I know Liv but you can't just take them."

"Actually I had no choice. When I went back in the living room she was passed out and she had a bottle of vodka next to her."

Jake couldn't believe what he was hearing, "That's unbelievable."

"I wrote her a note and put it next to her. I'll go there tomorrow and check on her but I don't like the way she's treating those kids."

"I know you don't Liv but you have to take them back tomorrow." She shook her head and walked back into the living room.

"Mommy, are they staying here with us?" asked Lea.

"They'll be with us tonight." "Yay!!" she screamed.

*F*orty-four

The next day, Olivia got up early and wanted to make breakfast for the kids. She went to check on them and they were already out in the living room playing.

"Good morning everyone, I'm going to start making breakfast soon. Don't make too much of a mess." Olivia walked in the nursery and checked on the babies and they were lying in their crib moving around. She quickly fed them, changed them and put them back in the crib. She went back in the kitchen and there was Jake already starting breakfast. "Thanks Jake."

"You're welcome beautiful," and he kissed her.

"After breakfast I'm going to go to Joy's mother's house and talk to her."

"You're going by yourself?"

"I can do things by myself Jake."

"Not with Joe out there on the loose, who knows what he's capable of. We'll take the kids to the neighbors and have them watch them for a little. I'm sure they won't mind."

"Okay Jake, if that's what you think." They ate breakfast and got the kids ready and took them to the neighbors. They got in the car and went to Joy's mothers.

When they arrived they saw the door open.

"Did you leave the door open yesterday?"

"No, of course I didn't."

"Liv get behind me." Jake grabbed his gun from his back and held it as they walked slowly to the house. When they got to the door, Jake yelled, "Anyone in there? Ms. Monroe?" But no sounds came from the house. He opened the screen door and started to enter through the front door.

"Jake be careful," Olivia whispered. He went in the living room and it was clear. Olivia was behind him the whole time. They walked through the kitchen and then walked down the hallway. They checked the bedroom where the kids were and it was clear. They went to the master bedroom and Jake slowly opened the door and had his gun drawn. He looked in and saw Ms. Monroe on the bed with her throat cut.

"Get back Liv."

"Why what do you see? I want to see." She tried to get through the door but she couldn't get in. She glanced and saw Joy's mom covered in blood. Olivia started screaming.

"Liv let's go, I have to call this in." They waited in the living room until the police and ambulance arrived.

Olivia said to Jake, "It has to be Joe."

"We don't know for sure yet Liv." "How could you say that? Joy was murdered and now her mother is dead. I need to get home to the kids." They made their statements and headed home.

"Liv are you alright?"

"I just feel so awful and there was so much blood. We have to hold on to Joy's kids and care for them. Joe is out here and he's coming for me. I know he is."

When they arrived home, they picked up the kids from the neighbors and went in their house and locked the doors. She called her parents to let them know what happened with Joy's mother and told them to be safe and keep their doors locked at all times. They tried to be as calm and strong as possible, especially for the kids. Olivia felt like she needed to tell Ethan and Hope the circumstances with their mom and grandmother.

"Jake could you take the kids to the playroom. I think it's time I talk to Ethan and Hope."

He squeezed her hand, "Are you sure you want to do that alone?"

She looked at him longingly, "They trust me." He let go of her hand and he took the kids to the playroom. Olivia looked at Ethan, "You and Hope are going to stay here so we can talk okay?" They both shook their heads and sat down on the couch. "Now listen to me very carefully, I am here for the both of you and we care about you very much. I wanted to let you know that something happened."

"What happened?" asked Hope.

"Well your mommy and grandmother are no longer with us."

"What do you mean no longer with us, what does that mean?" asked Ethan.

"It means they're no longer with us physically, they passed away." Ethan started to have tears in his eyes and Hope copied whatever he was doing.

"They're dead?"

"I'm so sorry for the both of you," and they went to her and hugged her tightly and cried. Olivia picked them up and took them to her bed and they passed out. Jake was coming down the hallway as Olivia was coming out of the bedroom.

"Is everything okay?" asked Jake. Olivia shook her head and he followed her to the living room.

"They didn't take it well, they both cried of course. Then they latched themselves to me before passing out so I took them to our bed."

"I figured that's what would happen," said Jake.

"I'm exhausted I think I'm going to just sleep on the couch," said Olivia.

In the middle of the night she woke up and Ethan was standing over her, "What's wrong?"

"I can't sleep."

"Okay come on I'll come and lay down with you for awhile until you fall asleep." She got up and walked to the bedroom and got into the bed. Ethan lay next to her and Hope was on the other side of her. She fell asleep with them in her arms.

*F*orty-five

*I*n the morning she woke up and the kids were gone. She got up out of bed, went to the nursery and the babies were stirring. She fed them and changed them and put them back in their cribs. She walked into Lea and Elijah's room and they weren't in there. She wandered down the hallway and into the living room and saw all of them with Jake on the couch watching cartoons.

"Hey what's going on in here?"

"Hey mommy we're watching cartoons."

"I see that. Did daddy make breakfast?"

"I was just about to." He got up and went into the kitchen and she followed him in.

"Is everything alright?"

"Yeah they woke up and piled around me when I was asleep on the couch so I woke up and put some cartoons on for them." She smiled at him.

There was a knock on the door, "Who could that be so early in the morning?" Olivia went to the door and opened it, "Can I help you?"

"Are you Mrs. Harrison?"

"Yes, can I help you?"

"I'm Claudia Hawthorne with Social Services. I'm here for Ethan and Hope Anne."

"Oh please come in. I was hoping we could take the children for now."

"I'm sorry Mrs. Harrison but we can't do that, they belong to the state now."

"Please call me Olivia. What if we wanted to take them?"

"You would have to take that up with the agency. Could you please get them ready for me?"

"Oh sure of course, please wait here."

Olivia went into the kitchen, "Who's that?"

"Its social services, they're here to take Ethan and Hope."

"Liv, you knew that would happen."

"I know I just feel terrible about it." She walked into the living room. "Okay Ethan and Hope, listen to me, you have to go with this nice woman but I'll see you soon."

"I don't want to go with that woman I want to stay here with you," said Ethan.

"Yeah," said Hope.

"We'll see each other very soon, I promise." She got them ready and walked them outside to Claudia's car. They got in and as they drove away, she waved with tears in her eyes. When she couldn't see them anymore she turned and went back into the house.

"Mommy, where did they go?" asked Lea.

"They had to leave us for awhile but we'll see them soon."

"Okay mommy." Olivia decided now would be a good time to finish the book that she started working on a few years ago about her ordeal she went through with Joy. The memories started to flow right back in because of Joe coming back in the picture.

The morning had come and gone and Jake came in to check on her.

"Are you doing alright in here Liv?"

"Yeah I'm just wrapping up for now, I'll finish it later. How are the kids doing?"

"They're doing fine, I fed and changed the twins and I took care of Lea and Elijah."

"Thanks babe."

That night as they were sleeping, Olivia kept on tossing and turning. She felt like she needed to keep on writing so she got up and went to the office and sat down and started to write. When morning came she couldn't believe she made a huge dent in the book. She was almost finished with it. She was exhausted when she saw the light peaking in through the window.

She went back to her bed and saw Jake getting up, "You're up early."

"I didn't sleep; I was up all night writing my book. I just couldn't get it out of my head."

"You should try and get some sleep baby; I'll take care of the kids."

"Are you sure Jake?"

"Yes ma'am, I got this." Olivia fell fast asleep. She dreamt the whole time about Ethan, Hope Anne, and Ms. Monroe laying there in a pool of blood. She woke up covered in sweat. "Wow that dream was insane," she said to herself. She got up out of bed and went out to the living room. The kids and the twins were out there in the playpen.

"Hi babies."

"Mommy's awake," yelled Lea. She climbed up on Olivia's lap and hugged her.

"How did you sleep?" asked Jake.

"I slept okay, except for a crazy dream. I feel like I should continue my book."

"I'll support you if you want to finish it."

"Thanks so much, I really want to." She got something to eat and drink and went back into the office and started writing. It was like she was possessed and she couldn't stop writing.

By midnight, she finally finished the book. She felt proud but emotionally drained because of everything that happened. She left the office and went to see Jake and he was passed out on the couch with the twins. She picked up the babies and took them back to their cribs. She woke Jake up and helped him to the bedroom. As he hit the bed he passed out. Olivia went to check on the kids and they were out cold. She climbed into bed with Jake and fell asleep immediately.

*F*orty-six

*W*hen she woke up in the morning she made breakfast for everyone. She went to the nursery and checked on the babies to feed them and change them. When she was finished, she woke up the kids and went to wake up Jake to let him know breakfast was ready.

"Good morning sunshine," she said. He pulled her into bed with him and held her tightly. "Come on breakfast is ready. I have to set the kids up in their chairs," she laughed. They both got up and went into the kitchen. The kids were waiting for their food. Olivia served them and she sat down. Jake came in and got himself breakfast and sat down with her.

"So what's on the agenda for today? Are you going to finish your book? You were working on it late last night."

She smiled at him, "I actually finished it today and I'm going to call Daniel."

"Wow really you finished it? That's great? How do you feel about it?"

"I feel really good about it."

"I mean how do you really feel about it?"

"It was tough but I got through it. It was a horrible time but I have these wonderful kids here now so I'm grateful for that."

When she was done with breakfast she went to get dressed and she called Daniel. He was very excited about it; he wanted to meet up with her about it. They planned to get together later that day so she could give it to him.

Later that day Olivia and Jake went to meet up with Daniel. They dropped the kids off at her parents. When they arrived Daniel was waiting for them.

"Hello Olivia it's nice to see you again."

"You too Daniel and this is my husband."

"It's nice to meet you," and he shook his hand. They sat down and discussed the book. She gave it to him and he provided a check for $5,000. "If it becomes a huge seller you could see a lot more Olivia." She signed some papers and the meeting was over.

"I hope they really like the book."

"I'm sure they will Liv, you have nothing to worry about."

When they got home from picking up the kids, Olivia felt a sense of relief that she was finally done the book and she handed if off to Daniel. She hoped it would be a success and a story for other women out there that went through the same ordeal.

A few days later she received a phone call from Daniel.

"We need to meet right away Olivia, we can meet at the same place if you want, say in like an hour?"

"Sure of course, see you then."

She hung up the phone, "Who was that?" asked Jake.

"It was Daniel; he wants to meet with me at the café in an hour. I'm afraid Jake, what if he didn't like it?"

"Don't be Liv; I'm sure it's fine. Just listen to what he has to say." The hour flew by and she kissed Jake and the kid's goodbye and headed to the café.

When she arrived Daniel was waiting for her at the same table as before.

She walked over and he stood up, "Thanks for meeting me in such short notice."

"Sure it's no problem, I hope everything is alright."

"Alright, it's more than alright, it's great!"

She smiled brightly, "Really? They liked it?"

"Oh Olivia not only did they like it, they loved it. They wanted me to give you this." He pulled out an envelope from his pocket and he slid it across the table. She picked it up and opened it. It was a check for $25,000.

"What is this?"

"That's from the publishing company. It's the earnings that you made for the book. They want you to do a book tour."

"Oh my God, I don't even know what to say."

"Say you'll do it and you're going to need an agent. Lucky for you I could be yours."

"Really, you have the credentials for that?"

"Believe it or not, that's what I was before I started working at the publishing company."

"Daniel I would love for you to be my agent, you've done so much for me already."

"You're going to be so successful Olivia, just wait and see. If you don't mind I have more papers for you to sign about the book tour and of course me being your agent."

Olivia smiled wide, "I can't believe this is happening to me."

"You should believe it, you deserve it." She signed the papers, they discussed his fee and she left with check in hand.

*F*orty-seven

*W*hen she got home she had a huge smile on her face.

"I'm home," she yelled out. Jake and the kids welcomed her home with a hug.

"So how did it go?"

"I have great news, my book, they loved it. They want me to do a book tour."

"Olivia that's so wonderful, I'm so happy for you," he picked her up and hugged her.

"When does that start?"

"I'm not sure yet, they're going to call me with all the details. I made Daniel my agent and I'm giving him fifteen percent of what I earn when I'm out on the road doing the tour."

"Okay that sounds fair," said Jake.

"I need to call my parents and tell them the good news." She got on the phone and dialed the number but it just rang and rang. "That's odd the answering machine didn't come on."

"Maybe try her cell phone?" She dialed the number and it just went right to voicemail.

"That's strange it just went right to voicemail. What if something happened to them?"

"I'll call a car to go over there and check on them, okay?"

"Thanks Jake, if you don't mind." He radioed a car to go out to her parent's house. Meanwhile, she sat on the couch and waited. Jake's cell phone started to ring. He picked it up and his face changed from normal to glum. Olivia looked at him, "What's wrong?" she cried.

He hung up the phone and turned to her, "Listen to me very carefully…"

She interrupted him, "Oh my God, they're dead aren't they?"

"Olivia they're not dead. When the officer got there he knocked on the door and there was no answer but he said something was strange so he tried the door and it opened. He saw your parents lying there barely breathing so he called an ambulance. They're on their way to the hospital."

Olivia was sobbing hard, "We have to get to the hospital."

"Of course, you get the kids dressed; I'll get the twins ready."

When they got to the hospital they ran to the desk, "I'm looking for my parents, Caroline and Nathan Mallor."

She looked on the computer, "They're in recovery; I'll get the doctor for you." They sat down in the waiting room and waited for the doctor to come out.

Finally one appeared, "Are you Olivia Mallor?"

"Yes, how are my parents?"

"They're both in stable condition but they're in and out of consciousness."

"Can I see them?"

"I would recommend that only you go and see them."

"Okay that's fine," she turned to Jake. "I'll be right back, okay?" He shook his head and he sat down with the kids. The doctor showed her the room and she walked in. She gasped as soon as she saw them. She went to her mom, "I'm so sorry mom," she whispered.

Her mom opened her eyes, "Olivia is that you?"

"Oh mom, how are you feeling? Are you okay?"

"I feel sore, like I got hit by a bus. Where is your father?"

"He's right next to you mom in the other bed. Do you know what happened to you?"

"I don't know, one minute we were laughing watching TV and the next we ended up here."

"Mom, I'm so sorry."

"Honey it's not your fault."

"I'm going to check on dad." She walked to her dad's bed and he was lying there with his eyes closed. She squeezed his hand but he didn't squeeze back.

"Is he okay?" asked her mom.

She walked back over to her, "I think he's sleeping. The doctor said that you both would be in and out of consciousness.

Just then the nurse came in, "I think it's time you let them rest. You can come back tomorrow."

Olivia shook her head at the nurse, "I'll see you tomorrow," she kissed her mom and she walked over to her father and kissed him and then she left the room.

When she got back to the waiting room the kids were sleeping and Jake was eagerly waiting.

When he saw her he stood up, "Is everything okay?"

"Yeah I talked to my mom but she didn't know what happened and my dad was still unconscious."

"I'm so sorry Liv."

"I feel like this is my entire fault," she said.

He looked at her and lifted her chin so his eyes could meet hers, "Don't ever say that, ever, you didn't do anything. Maybe we should have a cop watching the house."

"Good idea," said Olivia. "Let's get these kids home to bed."

When they got to the house they opened the door and there was a note on the floor, like someone pushed it under the door. Olivia picked up the piece of paper, lifted it open, and it read 'YOU'RE NEXT!' Jake looked at it and he immediately called it in. He checked the house and it was clear. He put the kids to bed. Olivia took the twins and put them in their cribs. There was a knock on the door, Jake went to look and it was the officer he works with. He told him the whole story and gave them the note. "We'll patrol the area and we'll have a cop out front. He thanked him and went to Olivia who was sitting on the couch.

"I can't believe this is happening to us."

"Liv, don't beat yourself up, it's not your fault."

"I know but it's affecting everyone around me. Joy is gone and so is her mother. My parents are badly hurt and in the hospital. I'm so afraid that something is going to happen to you or the kids."

"Don't worry Liv. We have cops patrolling the area and we have an officer out front. I think you should try and get some sleep."

"Good idea," she kissed him tenderly and she pulled him up and took him to bed.

Forty-eight

Olivia felt like something was wrong. She woke up and got up out of bed and went to check on the twins and the kids. She walked down the hallway and went in the nursery and they were sleeping peacefully. She left the room and went to the other kids rooms and they were sleeping as well. Still she felt like something was off. She walked in the kitchen and got a glass of water. When she was finished the water, she happened to look down and there was broken glass and dirt on the floor. She started to panic and was about to run but then hands grabbed her from behind. She was about to scream when Joe put his hands over her mouth.

"You knew you were going to be next Liv." He looked her up and down, "Mmm you still look hot."

Olivia looked scared to death, "How did you get in here?"

"I guess your husband didn't look well enough. I was here the whole time. Your body still looks amazing." He put her up against the wall and grabbed duct tape from his bag that he had with him and taped her mouth shut. He grabbed some rope and bound her hands together. "That should hold you for now, so what should I do with you?" He stood there for a while looking at her, licking his lips. He was inches from her, he slowly reached up and touched her face but she turned away. He slapped her in the face and then he slid his hands down to her chest. He untied her robe and pulled it open to reveal her naked body. "Man, do they look nice." He started cupping her and he bent down and started kissing them and sucking on them. Tears were streaming down her face as she was trying to tell to him to stop. "You don't like that Liv?" She shook her head. "Maybe you'll like this," he stuck his hand down further to cup her but she started to whimper. "Just like old times." He put his finger inside her and she winced. He withdrew his fingers and turned her around to face the wall. He bent her forward and forced himself inside of her and she started to cry out. All of a sudden he let go and there was an arm around Joe's head. It was Jake; he pushed Joe backwards and punched him in the gut. Joe fell back but he came back just as quickly to punch Jake. He got on top of Jake and started to choke him, he couldn't breathe. Olivia got in Joe's face to beg him to stop. He looked at her and let go of him. "He didn't tell you, did he?" He pulled the tape from her mouth, "Now don't scream, otherwise I'll have to put this back on."

Olivia shook her head and looked at Joe, "Tell me what?"

Joe laughed, "He was in on it?"

"What do you mean he was in on it, no way, were you Jake?" She looked at him scared to death. Jake looked at her and Olivia knew. She started to scream.

"I told you not to scream." He started to place the tape over her mouth but she pulled away.

"How could you do this me Jake? I trusted you, I loved you, we got married and I had your children."

"Liv, I swear it wasn't meant to happen this way. Yes I was in on it with Chris and Joe but just as quickly as I was in on it I dropped them because I fell in love with you."

"You got Sarah and Chris out didn't you and you even helped with Joe's release."

Joe was smiling, "You've got a good man their Liv."

"Chris and Sarah got out themselves. I had nothing to do with that, and with Joe that was just luck. I had nothing to do with that either. I told you Liv I fell in love with you. You're my whole world."

"I don't know if I can even believe you."

"Olivia, trust me, I met these guys years ago and I had no idea that they targeted you until it already happened. When I met you, everything changed. I fell in love with you and your kids." Olivia sat there dumbfounded and was crying.

"Well isn't that sweet, sorry Liv, but I have to do what I came here to do." He pulled back the tape over her mouth. Jake then bum rushed him and Joe fell backwards. Joe got on top of Jake and punched him in the face and started to strangle him. "Really dude, this is how it's going to be? I can't believe over a girl too." Olivia made the split decision and fell on top of him; she was shaking her head uncontrollably at Joe. "What's it to you?" He pulled back the tape, I'll do whatever you want me to do just please don't hurt him. He pulled the tape back over her mouth. He went back to his bag and grabbed more rope and tied up Jake. He grabbed the duct tape and put it over his mouth. "You might want to watch this buddy." He perked Jake up. He grabbed Olivia and placed her on the floor next to Jake. He started to grab at her naked body and put a finger inside her, she lay there crying. Jake watched in horror what was happening to his wife, he couldn't move. He got on top of her and forced his way inside her again, he started to moan. "Your wife feels so good."

Just then Elijah came in, "Mommy what's going on?" Joe peeled back and pulled his pants up.

"Oh hey little guy, we were just playing." Elijah looked over at Jake and he knew something was wrong; he started to run to the front door. "I'm sorry little buddy, I can't let you leave."

"Why not, what are you doing to my mommy and daddy?"

"I told you we're playing a little game. Now is there anymore of you back there." He looked at Olivia and she shook her head no. "Don't look at her boy, you can tell me the truth I won't hurt them." Elijah shook his head no. Joe took his little hands and tied them up, "It's all a part of the game."

*F*orty-nine

*W*hat Joe didn't know was that Lea was lurking around and she saw what was happening. She quickly gathered the twins and she snuck out the back sliding doors that were in her parent's room. She quickly went to her neighbor's house and banged on the door. The door finally opened and Mrs. Crovavich was standing there in her robe.

"Good God child what are you doing out here in this late hour with the babies?"

"Please Mrs. Crovavich, my parents and my brother is being held captive by a man. You need to tell the officer that's out front of my house."

She looked at her strangely, "Are you sure?"

"Yes I'm sure, please hurry." She went out her front door and let the officers know that there was someone in the house.

Meanwhile back in the house, Joe didn't know what to do in the situation he was in because now there was a child involved. He walked to the back of the house and looked in the bedrooms and there was no one in there so he walked back even further to the nursery. He looked in the cribs and they were both empty. He went into the living room and saw a family photo. He stopped when he saw in the photo a girl with dark hair that looked just like Olivia and him.

He came back in the kitchen and looked at Olivia, "Who is this?" He pulled off her tape, "And don't lie to me." She looked at Jake, "Don't look at him. Tell me who she is or I swear to God I'll kill your son."

"Okay Okay, it's my daughter Lea," Olivia cried. "Does she belong to me?" It never occurred to Olivia that Lea could be Joe's child. He did rape her a few times.

She stammered, "I don't know." He looked at the photo and then put it in front of Olivia's face. "Look at the picture! There's a striking resemblance, don't you think?" Olivia couldn't deny it. She looked almost identical to Joe. "There is a nursery in the back with two cribs but no babies. Where are my daughter and the two babies?"

Olivia had tears in her eye, "They're away at my Aunt Stephanie's."

"How come he's not with the rest of the kids?"

"He wasn't feeling good, so he stayed home."

"You better be telling me the truth."

"I am," she whispered. He huffed and puffed and walked back and forth. He picked up Olivia and took her to the bedroom that she shared with Jake.

"You better not be lying to me sweetheart."

"I'm not Joe."

"That's a good girl. Chris used to tell me that you used to go down on him pretty good so I want you to do that for me." She looked at him with disgust.

He unzipped his pants and pushed her down on her knees, "Please don't do this Joe."

"Do it now before I go and do something you don't want me to do." She didn't want to but she had an idea. She opened her mouth and he slid into her; he was groaning and pushing himself deeper into her mouth. She knew right then and there that she had to make a snap decision, so she bit down hard. He screamed and he fell down.

Olivia got up and ran into the kitchen, "Come on we have to go, now!" She helped Jake up and she took Elijah and ran out the door. They ran right into the officer who was about to knock on the door, "He's inside, Joe's inside." Just then a whole bunch of officers showed up, they told them the whole story. After she was done telling them the story the officers went inside.

Just then Lea came out of the neighbors house, "Oh my God Lea, I was wondering where you were," she hugged her tightly. "Where are the twins?"

"They're in the house with Mrs. Crovavich." When the officers took Joe out Olivia cried and turned to Jake.

"Liv, I'm so sorry." She looked at him, "You tried to save my life and for that I'm grateful. It's going to take a long time to even forgive you."

"Of course Liv and I promise every day I'll make it up to you. I never wanted to hurt you." She didn't say anything else to him.

She walked over to Lea and bent down, "I can't believe you did that Lea, you're a very brave girl."

"I think we've been through enough mommy."

"I couldn't agree more."

THE END

20288505R00210

Printed in Poland
by Amazon Fulfillment
Poland Sp. z o.o., Wrocław